I0642758

SHADOW'S WRATH

THE SHADOW HUNT SERIES
BOOK 3

IAN FORTEY
AND
RON RIPLEY

EDITED BY ANNE LAO
AND DAWN KLEMISH

ISBN: 979-8-89476-283-8
Copyright © 2025 by ScareStreet.com

ENTER THE REALM OF TERROR...

We'd like to take a moment to thank you for your support and invite you to join our VIP newsletter.

Dive deeper into the darkness with exclusive offers, early access to new releases, and bone-chilling deals when you sign up at www.ScareStreet.com.

Let the nightmares begin…

See you in the shadows,
Scare Street

PROLOGUE

Sweat dripped from Harlan's face. He stood up, feeling a slight burn after his final set of leg extensions, and used a towel to wipe down the machine. There was something satisfying about doing workouts so late at night.

He used to go in the afternoon but found the place too crowded. He didn't like waiting for machines or listening to people talking on their cell phones while they made videos about their workouts to post on social media.

Since he started hitting the gym just after one o'clock in the morning, he found it much more relaxing. There were three or four other people in the building at most, aside from Ned at the front desk.

Every machine was available, no one made videos, and no one bothered him. Workouts were less stressful and more satisfying. He was happy.

Harlan had been divorced for four years and had not had a successful date in that time. That didn't mean he hadn't gone on dates; they had just all ended badly. He was not good at talking to women about things they cared about, and he understood most of that was his fault. If he wasn't talking about his ex, he talked about video games or his favorite microbrews. Eventually, he realized he needed to do something if he hoped to progress.

Part of his self-improvement journey included working out. He tried half the gyms in Albany before he found one he liked. Since then, he'd gone regularly for nine months and was happy with the results. There were times early on when he felt like quitting, but he forced himself to keep at it. He lost weight, looked better, and felt better. Things were going well.

The most stressful part of his new workout routine was trying to avoid telling his mother what he did all day. He made the mistake of mentioning the hour that he went to the gym once, and she spent a week worrying that he would be mugged in the parking lot. His mother was positive that as soon as the sun went down, criminals came out like vampires and preyed on anyone foolish enough to not be barred indoors.

After returning the machine to the way he had found it, Harlan headed to the locker room. Another bonus of being in the gym so late was that he could shower for as long as he wanted without worrying that someone would go through his stuff. Someone had stolen his shoes while he was in the shower at a decent hour before.

By the time he was ready to leave, it was just after two in the morning. His goal had never been to turn himself into Mr. Universe, and he wasn't trying to bulk up. He just wanted to feel good about himself and attract women. He wasn't ugly, but he had a gut when he started, and that wasn't doing him any favors.

Harlan packed his stuff in a duffel bag and waved goodbye to Ned at the door before heading outside. It had been a hot day, but the night was oddly cool for this time of year. It felt nice after being at the gym for so long.

His SUV was parked about ten yards from the gym entrance, in front of an audiologist's office. There were only four other vehicles in the lot, and one had parked next to him. He hated it when that happened.

The van parked next to his vehicle looked like an unfortunate relic from the eighties. One of those big, nondescript vehicles with no side windows that could have been a delivery vehicle or something the FBI sat in the back of to spy on the mob.

Harlan could see no one in the van, but whoever owned it needed to take it through a car wash. The white paint was almost impossible to see halfway up the sides thanks to the mud splatters. The rest of it was dull and grimy.

The van had parked too close to his vehicle, with tires right on the yellow line that separated parking spaces. He cursed the driver quietly and squeezed between the vehicles to open his rear door and toss in his duffel bag. A whole parking lot with hundreds of empty places, and this guy had to park right next to him.

Harlan's hand was on the handle of the driver's side door when the dirty white van's sliding door flew open with a loud, rickety rumble. Two masked men grabbed him and pulled him roughly into the back of the van.

"What the hell—"

A rag was jammed into his mouth, stifling any more words as he was thrust onto the bare metal surface of the van's interior. A third man, his face uncovered to expose a wrinkled face that looked tired but determined, put a hand on Harlan's chest and jammed a syringe into his neck.

Harlan struggled, trying to fight the three men off and spit out the rag so he could call for help. The door slammed shut, and the van's engine rumbled to life. Drowsiness overcame him quickly as the van began to move. He resisted whatever they had given him, but his limbs felt heavy, and it was hard to focus. The man who injected him said something, but the words had no meaning.

Lights passed by, sending shadows through the van. Harlan couldn't focus on any of it.

✳✳✳

Harlan coughed. The taste of the rag was still in his mouth, although the rag itself was gone. It tasted sour. The smell around him was worse. It was like roadkill on a warm day, but the air was also dense with an oddly cool humidity. It felt thick like the gym, but clammy at the same time. Mold and meat and vomit were layered like a putrid cocktail. He coughed again.

"What...?"

It was the first thing he could think to say. He was in the dark. He had been at the gym. He remembered doing his workout. He remembered taking a shower and then…

What happened next?

He had a vague recollection of a dirty, white van. His memory was hazy about what had happened. Someone must have taken him, but why?

He was in the dark on a cold, damp floor. It was gritty, like a basement. The smell of the air was revolting, and the more he moved about, the more he felt his stomach heave. In the dark, he wondered what the dampness was. Was it just water or something else? There was a slimy feeling on his fingers, and he tried not to focus on it.

Harlan tried to get to his feet but wobbled and fell over. His head swam from the effort, and he realized someone had drugged him. It was still in his system.

"Hello?" he yelled, lying on his side, and feeling the dampness soak into his clothing. "Help me! Somebody help, please!"

He sat up again, slowly, and leaned back against the wall, his heart racing. He took a moment to catch his breath and heard a door open to his left. No light came in, but there was a rush of air. It was slightly warmer than the room and carried a heavier stench. He suppressed a gag.

"Who's there?" he said in the darkness. "What do you want?"

Footsteps preceded a silhouette coming toward him. As his eyes adjusted, he made out the shape of a man.

Harlan looked up and focused on the face in front of him. It was a man, but it was too dark to make out his features very well.

"My name is Roy," the man in the dark said. His voice was soft but sounded old. It had a gravelly tone like Harlan's grandfather, though the two sounded nothing alike otherwise. "Some people call me the Houndmaster, though that won't mean much to you."

"What do you want? Why are you doing this?" Harlan demanded. His muscles felt so weak, and his head swam when he moved too quickly. He felt like he could sleep for a day. "Where am I?"

"I apologize for the rough treatment, Harlan. It is a necessary part of the process. My work requires subjects, and volunteers are in short supply. Rest assured, you will be part of something magnificent. Something unknown in human history," Roy said, his voice gentle and reassuring.

"What are you talking about? Who are you?" Harlan demanded.

"Harlan, please understand. I have made remarkable breakthroughs with my work these past weeks. I have a method of almost guaranteed results. Perfect transference and construction nearly one hundred percent of the time. It's unheard of."

Harlan shook his head, not understanding what the man was talking about.

"Please, just let me go."

"You don't understand because you have no context, and I appreciate that. You should think of it like making sourdough. Have you ever made sourdough?" Roy asked.

"What?" Harlan asked, baffled.

"Sourdough bread. Are you familiar?"

"Of course," Harlan answered.

"Wonderful. A good sourdough requires a starter. That was what I didn't understand before. You need a bit of the end at the beginning, you see. What you desire must be made from what you desire, so I use the old to make the new, and it has been beyond my wildest dreams."

"God, please, I don't know what you're talking about. Please, just let me go."

Roy chuckled in the dark.

"No, no, you wouldn't know, would you? I'm explaining myself as if you've been here for weeks. I am sorry again, Harlan. I usually work alone. I don't have to explain myself often. Let me just show you."

Roy shifted his position, turned to face the door, and whistled loudly. Moments later, a light moved from the hallway. At first, Harlan thought it was somebody coming with a flashlight in their hand.

Something lumbered into the room on all fours, and Harlan could see that the illumination came from the figure itself, as though it was glowing. It was a person. Or had been.

Harlan felt a scream freeze inside of him like a weight in his chest, and it refused to come out. The person—man or woman, he couldn't say—was nude and brutalized beyond description. Broken bone fragments jutted out through flesh across their back, shoulders, and chest.

The person walked on all fours, but neither their arms nor their legs bent in the way they should have. The inflamed, red flesh of their limbs looked like it had been boiled, and the bones were broken in multiple places. As they walked, Harlan could see bend after bend after bend, as though the arm had half a dozen new joints.

The face was what finally made the scream purge itself from Harlan's body. Someone had peeled the skin down to the bone in two perfect rectangular strips from the top of the being's bald head down the face and ending at the jawline. Each was wide enough to lay bare the empty eye sockets and the skeletal mouth and teeth, with a narrow band of unmarred flesh between which sat a normal nose. The exposed bone was so white that Harlan thought it might be fake.

Roy ignored Harlan's screams and continued talking as the glowing monstrosity ambled to his side and crouched next to him like a dog.

"I've learned that the process of creating the Hounds is best served by what I call a 'merging'. You need that starter. You use a fully formed success to kickstart your next creation. Please believe I wish this process did not have to be as painful as it is, but pain is as necessary as the merging."

He made a clicking sound, and the creature at his feet got up again. The empty eyes looked toward Harlan. It made no sense, but Harlan felt in his gut that it was watching him. The impossible, eyeless thing could see him.

It moved in Harlan's direction, and he scrambled backward, dizziness overtaking him as he flopped onto the floor. He screamed and sputtered as he distanced himself from the horrible thing.

"Please, no! Somebody, help me! Help me!" he screamed.

He felt a hand like ice close over his ankle. He tried to kick it but there was nothing to kick, like the revolting thing was made of mist. It pulled him back and then grabbed him with its other hand, taking hold of the back of his shirt and forcing him face down on the wet, slimy floor.

Harlan screamed and begged, but there was no way to fight the thing or get free from it. His feet passed through it when he kicked, and the hands might as well have been iron.

"That's good," Roy said as Harlan struggled. "It's good to fight. This is not a quick process. Fighting ensures that, when you break, it will be precise and thorough."

The old man turned to leave, and Harlan felt something cold and sharp pierce his back, pushing below the skin, into the muscle, and between his ribs. The pain was immense. It felt like the thing on his back had shoved a railroad spike into him.

All he could do was scream, even as he heard the door close behind him.

✳✳✳

Roy walked to the end of the hall. Harlan's screams were muffled, but he could still hear them. The Hound would not kill him; it was not instructed to do so. It knew that its job was to inflict pain but not so much that the man would not survive.

The process of making a Hound was still hit-or-miss, even with Roy's discoveries. The man had to be seasoned, which would take days or even weeks. But when he was ready, he would be broken, to return the way Mr. Shadow wanted him. He would come back as a Hound.

Roy opened the unlocked door at the end of the passage. The

darkness was all-encompassing, but he still felt the presence of the large, foreboding form within it.

"The newest transformation is underway. You can start the physical shaping any time you wish," he said to the darkness.

There was no answer, nor did he expect one. His only confirmation that he was heard would come when he checked in on Harlan next and saw which bones had been broken. Mr. Shadow spoke with actions far more than words.

CHAPTER 1
STRANGERS IN THE NIGHT

The deadbolt fell into place with a heavy click. James Moran stared out the window set into the glass door at the street beyond. Traffic was light, and just a handful of cars passed by the storefront.

It had been a slow day at work with only three customers coming into the shop. Most of his business was done electronically or over the telephone as many customers didn't want to be seen out and about looking for the things they desired. Not the ones who wanted his more obscure offerings.

Not for the first time, James wondered if he should close the brick-and-mortar and work out of his home. Just as quickly as the thought entered his mind, he pushed it away.

The shop had been in his family for a long time. There was a legacy to being part of Moran and Moran. Curating antiques, haunted or otherwise, was something he took pride in. Even if people were slow to come in, he still got satisfaction out of the work he did.

It was just as well that few people showed up that day. He was tired from spending several late nights trying to help Shane Ryan deal with the Harvesters. Try as he might, James could not get any solid information about them. It beggared belief that no one knew about a group of people charging money to hunt spirits, but he kept hitting brick walls.

The limited information he had discovered was not very helpful and didn't direct Shane toward anyone in charge. It was only through thinking creatively that James discovered several of the ghosts that were associated with the Harvesters. James had dealt with the spirits directly or indirectly in the past. Only a handful of them, but it was the best he could do.

He had feelers out and had let people he trusted know that he was interested in learning more, but all he could do was wait for them to come back to him with information. People who traveled in these circles, even ones who were trustworthy, were still often very tight-lipped. Life and death situations tended to breed secrecy.

James drew the blinds and swept the floor. He gave the glass surfaces a wipe down to get rid of any fingerprints that might have accumulated and then headed to the back of the store to do the day's accounting in his office.

His office was growing cluttered, and he resolved to tidy it up soon. He had promised himself that more than once, of course, and still hadn't gotten around to it. Instead of worrying about it just then, he filled a small electric kettle with water and set it to boil so he could have tea while he worked.

No sooner had he started going through the receipts for the day when the phone rang. Despite being after hours, he still answered it, hoping there was a potential lead that he could pass on to Shane.

Although he was not involved with the Harvesters, James still felt a degree of responsibility. It was the ghost of a man named August that had come to James in fear of them that had gotten Shane involved. And, since many of the ghosts the Harvesters hunted had either come from James or were owned by previous customers, he felt indirectly responsible for what happened to them.

He answered the phone on the third ring.

"James Moran," the voice on the phone said.

He did not recognize the voice, but it was not asking a question. They spoke clearly in a deep, raspy voice that sounded far away like someone was using the speakerphone from across the room.

"Yes, how can I help you?" James replied.

"You seek the Harvesters. I know where they come from."

"You do?" James quickly unearthed a pad of paper and a pen. "May I ask with whom I'm speaking?"

"Do you remember the name Ezra Deacon?"

The question was soft and breathy with a hint of expectation. James thought the name sounded familiar; in the way one recognized a person in an old photograph and can't quite place who it was. He'd heard it before but couldn't conjure a face or contact.

"I'm afraid I don't. Have we met?"

The voice sighed.

"I am not Ezra Deacon, Mr. Moran. Ezra Deacon died half a century ago."

James said nothing. Something came to mind then. Ezra Deacon was a man he had met as a child. He might have been a client of the business: James remembered his father introducing him to Deacon long ago. He could recall nothing about who Deacon was, though.

"That was well before my time," James replied.

"Was it?" the voice said, a hint of something playful in his reply.

"It was. How does Mr. Deacon relate to the Harvesters?" James asked. He was keenly aware the caller had avoided identifying himself, but he had something he wanted him to know about Deacon.

"It began with Ezra Deacon, James. Every moment. Every idea. Every death. It all began with Ezra Deacon."

"And how did you come to learn this so many years after his death?"

"I was there when he died," the voice explained. It spoke in little more than a whisper now.

"And you know that Deacon started the Harvesters?"

"I know everything," the voice whispered.

James had written Deacon's name on the pad of paper but nothing else. The voice on the phone made him uneasy, and he could not put his finger on why. What the caller was saying was potentially revelatory, but it was not shocking or even off-putting. He didn't know Deacon, and he had no connection to the man, but there was something in the voice. The cadence, the articulation of words, the timbre. Something in it put him on edge.

"It would help immensely if I knew who you were," James said.

"James," the voice breathed, almost an admonishment. "My name is Mr. Shadow. And I think you ought to start running."

Despite the breathy quality of the voice, James realized that whoever was speaking was not breathing over the phone. Shane had told James that someone or something calling itself Mr. Shadow was working with Beatrix and the Harvesters. Shane assumed it was a spirit, and James felt that was accurate.

"I'm not sure if running—" James began.

"You misunderstand me, James," Mr. Shadow said. "Run now. You need to run right now."

The ghost of a twenty-something-year-old man called Alec tumbled into the doorway just then, and the phone clicked as the line went dead. Alec spent most of his days leaning against the wall in front of the store.

He had been a fixture of Moran and Moran for years. He was a danger to no one, and he kept to himself, and James allowed him to hang out at his leisure. He wasn't a guard dog, and they didn't have a formal business relationship, but the ghost had alerted James to the presence of the odd spirit from time to time. It usually happened when clients brought in unsecured haunted items.

The ghost was in a wide-eyed panic, a state unlike any James had seen. If he could breathe, James had no doubt the ghost would be gasping for air as it looked like he had just sprinted to the back of the building.

"There's something outside," the ghost hissed, keeping his voice low as he looked toward the front of the building.

"What?" James asked, dropping the phone.

Alec's eyes darted nervously, and it was clear he was afraid. James had seen ghosts afraid. August had been afraid. But this was panic. This was the fear a person feels when they think their life is in danger. James had seen it on the faces of men in battle. He'd probably worn a similar expression when he was under fire. It was rare on a ghost, indeed.

"I don't know what it is."

The words hung in the air for a moment, and James tried to understand what the ghost could be speaking of.

"What do you mean?"

"I've never seen anything like it. It's not alive. It's a monster."

"A monster? What do—"

James was unable to finish the question. Something latched onto Alec's ankle and pulled him to the floor. From inside the office, James could only see the ghost lose his footing. It was a quick, forceful jerk that yanked the ghost off-balance and knocked him to the floor. A heartbeat later, he was pulled out of view.

Alec cried out as James got to his feet. It was two strides to the doorway and then James froze, looking toward the entrance to the shop area. Alec was on the ground, and above him was a ghost unlike anything James had seen or even imagined.

To call it a monster was not inaccurate. It had clearly been human once. James did not doubt that this was one of the Hounds Shane had told him about. Even after hearing the description, James had not been prepared for the reality.

What had once been a muscular man, possibly a bodybuilder based on his size, was now a patchwork of trauma and injury. It stood on all fours, and along the sides of its body, all its ribs seemed to be broken, the ends poking out through the flesh like a row of spikes along the flesh of a lizard.

The hulking man's knees had been broken and reset backward so his legs bent in the opposite direction as a living person. There was similar trauma in the arms. It looked as though someone had pulverized the ghost's elbows, and when James watched it move, the joints now worked

13

like a hinge, easily bending forward and backward.

The Hound's head had been shorn of hair. Someone with a skilled hand had then set about excising flesh in a precise and twistedly artistic fashion. They had turned the man into a jack-o'-lantern.

Two perfect, equilateral triangles were cut over the eyes, exposing empty, bony sockets within. Skin and muscle were cleaned away, and the bone was polished white. A smaller triangle was cut over the nose, removing skin and cartilage. Finally, the mouth was cut away in favor of a parody of a smile that stretched to the ghost's ears on either side. Devoid of lips, the skeletal grin and exposed teeth were all that remained.

The Hound held down Alec with one hand. The skeletal mouth chattered, and the teeth clicked together, but no sound came out. James, still in the doorway to his office, reached for the filing cabinet inside and closed his hands over an iron bar he had used as a paperweight for years.

The ghostly monstrosity chattered its teeth again, and James took a step forward out of the office, bringing down the iron bar on top of its head like a hammer. It was unable to react fast enough before the iron met ghost flesh.

The metal reacted to the spirit's body and immediately thrust it back to wherever it had come from. It was as though the ghost had never existed, blinking from the room without a sound.

"What the hell was that?" Alec gasped, scrambling to his feet.

"Like you said, a monster. And it's back," James replied.

The Hound passed through the front door of the shop. Wherever the haunted item was located, it was close by. Someone—Mr. Shadow or someone working for him—was nearby. They had brought the thing to kill James. He would do his best to make it work for that goal.

"Run," James advised.

"What about you?"

"I'll be fine. Run."

The ghost gritted his teeth as the Hound ambled forward on its oddly bending limbs. James wasted no more time on him and headed for the cellar door. He had little time and even less idea of what to do.

Chapter 2
Panic Room

The door at the bottom of the stairs was locked. James always kept it secure, and few people knew it existed. The basement beneath his shop was a secure facility for storing things he could not risk storing elsewhere. It served a variety of other purposes over the years, some less savory than others. Some of the secure rooms were locked as tightly as he could make them. The things within them could never get out, nor could anyone be allowed to enter.

One of the most useful things James had discovered, though he could not claim ownership of the idea, was lead-infused glass. The Cult of the Endless Night had made extensive use of it in their ghost zoos, putting spirits on display without having to worry about sealing their haunted items in lead boxes or bags of salt.

A ghost trapped behind lead glass could be seen and even spoken to, but it was as secure as if the haunted item was under lock and key. James had several such cells in his basement, a few of which were not occupied.

He was under no illusion that he could capture the Hound that was after him. Luring it into one of the lead glass cages would be next to impossible, and the only bait he had was himself. The last thing he wanted was to become trapped in a room with a ghost that couldn't escape. But that was not his only idea.

James unlocked the basement door and let himself in before sealing it securely behind him. It was not a lead door, and even if it was, the walls around it would not keep the ghost out. Whoever brought the ghost, however, might be looking for him. James would make sure they'd have to work to find him.

He turned down a hall to his left and passed several sealed rooms. The basement was larger than he needed, and a lot of the space was empty. Some of it was just storage: He kept some files and even old furniture tucked away down there. Some of the rooms held haunted items that he stored for clients, and a few held more dangerous items, with higher security than he could offer in the shop upstairs.

He kept the lead glass cells in the back hallway. Two were occupied, and he rarely went into those rooms. No one else knew about them, and no one but James knew what was in them. He had no interest in entering either of them now.

The first cell, however, held an empty cell.

James unlocked the door and let himself in. He looked back quickly and saw nothing in pursuit. The Hound had not made it down to him yet, so he still had time.

Nothing was remarkable about the glass cages. They looked like something that any zoo might have to keep an animal on display. Just simple, average-looking glass panels and a door with a locking mechanism.

The technology to make it was advanced enough that the glass had the same color and clarity as regular glass. Lower-quality stuff might be thicker and have a slight gray hue to it, but James did not pay for lower quality.

He grabbed two bottles of water from a cabinet near the door—there was one in every cell room in the basement—and the lone chair from inside the room. Once he had his supplies, he let himself into the cage. The door closed behind him and sealed, a security feature of each cell. No door could be mistakenly left open.

James reached into his pocket and pulled out his cell phone. He had only reached his contacts list when the partially flayed face of the Hound pushed through the wall and looked into the room.

The ghost's empty eyes fell upon James, and the two stared at one another. He set the phone on the chair next to him and waited. The walls, ceiling, and floor were paneled with reinforced glass. Short of the building collapsing on him, the ghost should not be able to reach him. In theory, at least.

The Hound stared at him from the door without moving for a long moment, and then, seemingly unprovoked, bounded forward.

James stood his ground and watched. There was nothing else to do but have faith in his plan. The deformed but muscular spirit crossed the room in just two strides of its broken limbs, and then, it leaped.

The lipless mouth parted, and the skeletal jaw hung wide open. It was on a collision path. The aim seemed clear. It would leap on James and close its teeth over his throat. But it never got that far.

The ghost's extended hands hit the glass first, and a vibration rang through the surface like a gentle tap with a cushioned stick. Not a thump or a ping, just a resonant hum.

James watched as the ghost's arms bent involuntarily, folding in on its body. The face hit, and all forward movement stopped as its head skidded across the surface.

The Hound's body followed suit. First the shoulder, then the arm, then the side until its hips made contact, and it tumbled to the ground.

It was clear the spirit had never encountered such glass. As James watched, it got to its feet and tried to push one of the glass walls out of its way. The ghost paced the length of the cage, testing each of the glass panels. There was no way inside.

The Hound made no noise, but it tried to dig under the glass and climb over it. It tried the door and the seams between the panels while James watched silently, observing how it worked.

The name "Hound", the look of the creature, and the way it moved in the obvious purpose with which it was sent all gave it bestial qualities. But it was still made from a man. The ghost must have had the properties of reason, even if it could no longer speak, and was turned into a broken monstrosity. No matter how intelligent it was, though, it could not overcome what it was and its weaknesses. Ghosts could not pass through lead.

James watched it closely, both repulsed and impressed. That someone could forge such a ghost seemed impossible, but he was seeing it. Shane had said there were many of them, each designed similarly. Formed from living subjects who were tortured to death in the hope that their ghost would manifest and display the practical attributes of the horrors the living subject had endured. It was a nightmare beyond compare.

"What was your name?" James asked, drawing the Hound's attention.

He crouched until he was eye to eye with the spirit with just the thin pane of glass between them, and stared into the empty sockets in its skull. He could see inside the spirit's head where the brain had once sat, now gone as a result of whatever torment the victim had endured.

James had no doubt the Hound saw him, even though there were no eyes or a brain. Spirits were beyond such physical necessities. It retained all the senses the man it was forged from had possessed in life. He wondered if it still felt the pain or had a memory of what had happened to it.

It was hard to imagine anyone enduring what this poor creature had. For it to be what it was, it must have lived until the point it became what James saw before him.

That meant the man, whoever he had been, had been alive when they broke his joints. He had been alive as they shattered his ribs and forced them through his flesh. He had been alive as they cut skin from his face in the caricature of a Halloween decoration.

Death must have come when they pulled out the brain. And in that moment, the ghost had been created. James had never heard of anything so cruel and inhuman. The fact that it had been successful multiple times was too terrible a thought to entertain. So many of the victims must have died on the spot; others would have died before they got to that point.

And yet more, if they returned as ghosts, might have only returned as they looked in life. Dozens upon dozens dead so someone could create custom nightmares.

"You need not do this," James told the Hound. "Whatever they did to you, whatever they forced you to endure, you can be free of it now. You have that power."

James was not necessarily as sympathetic to ghosts as someone like Frank Benedict was. He couldn't say for certain if he would be as harsh sometimes as Shane Ryan was, either. He was pragmatic. Like people, ghosts were a mixed bag. Some were tolerable and some were not. But no one, living or dead, deserved what had happened to this nameless, nearly faceless man.

The Hound chattered its teeth. James doubted it could communicate. He wondered if the human victim had retained his sanity before death. It seemed unlikely. And if that was the case, the mind of the Hound could be a scrambled, unreachable thing. It was likely better off being destroyed. That would be the only true freedom for it, but it was a freedom that James could not provide.

People were waiting for the Hound to return. Someone had brought it to James' shop. If Mr. Shadow was a ghost, it wasn't him. There were human servants, Harvesters, doing the legwork for him. They were outside somewhere, and if the ghost didn't return, there was a good chance they would come looking. The lead glass cage could not keep out the living.

If James had had more time to prepare, he could have better armed himself. He could have come up with a defense, but he had reacted hastily. He only had one weapon left.

He retrieved his phone from where he had set it down and pulled up the contact list once more. The Hound watched him keenly with empty eyes as he scrolled and found the number for Shane Ryan.

"Hello?"

Shane's voice sounded gravelly like James had awoken him, even though it was not that late in the evening.

"Shane, it's James Moran. I'm trapped in the basement of the shop, looking at one of your Hounds."

"You gotta be kidding," Shane replied.

"I'm quite serious," James continued. "I suspect Harvesters are close by. I'm not sure how long I can hold them off."

"What's the Hound doing now?" Shane asked.

"Looking right at me."

Shane set the cup of coffee he had been drinking on the step next to him. He was behind the house, sitting on the stairs that led to the back door, watching the garden. He found it peaceful in the early evening, especially as the sun was setting, to watch the light fade beyond the horizon in a way that lit up the garden.

It had been just more than a week since Beatrix died. He had spent that time recovering from his injuries and getting the rest he needed to regain his strength. He was not at one hundred percent yet, and his face had blossomed with a series of bruises that made him look like he'd been hit by a truck, but he felt better.

Beatrix, who he had once thought was the leader of the Harvesters, had broken into his home. She had planned to kill him, but she had become unhinged as well. She was not acting as rationally as she should have been, and when the ghosts of the house distracted her, she fell into their trap.

She died in the root cellar beneath the house, murdered not just by the Dark Ones but by Carl, Eloise, and the Davis sisters. When he had gone to retrieve her body, there was nothing there. The Dark Ones refused to tell him what happened to her, but he had no doubt that she was dead.

"Can you hold it off while I drive down there?" Shane asked.

"I'm in one of the lead glass cells in the basement. It can't get in," James said.

Shane was on his feet, heading through the house toward the front door. James Moran's shop was a short drive from Nashua, but it would still take time to get there. If there were Harvesters around, or there was a weakness in the glass that the Hound could exploit, he would not reach James in time.

"How close are the Harvesters, you think?" Shane asked.

"I hit it with an iron bar. It was back in seconds. So, they have to be pretty close," James explained.

That made sense. In Shane's experience, the Harvesters were very mobile. He thought that, without Beatrix or Lanthimos to lead them, there would be nobody left, but he had obviously underestimated them.

Whoever Mr. Shadow was, the mysterious benefactor of the Harvesters and the one who fed Beatrix her information, he was still hard at work. Shane knew Shadow was a ghost, but not whose ghost. He also had no idea why Mr. Shadow was so invested in Beatrix's work.

The Harvesters had an endgame, and even without Beatrix, they were still after it. Now, it seemed, James Moran was part of that.

Agent Ventura had pointed out once already that many of the ghosts had a link to James, but neither Shane nor James made much of that fact. James had links to hundreds of ghosts, maybe more. Maybe there was a stronger link.

Shane left the house and got into his car, assuring James that he would be there as soon as he could. Whatever Harvesters were still at work were ones Shane had not encountered. He had assumed the operation was small enough that, if any others straggled about, they would have disbanded once Beatrix was gone.

That someone had attacked James made Shane wonder. Perhaps the Harvesters worked in cells like the Cult of the Endless Night had. Maybe there were others out there, each with their own Beatrix. It was a prospect he didn't look forward to learning more about.

He drove fast but not so fast that he would be pulled over. He didn't need to draw any more attention to himself or put James at any more risk.

Shane did not take his normal path to James' shop once he arrived in town. He chose a slightly more circuitous route, taking a side street that led him to the shop, which he drove past in the flow of traffic.

A handful of cars were still parked on the street, but the most notable was a white cube van, the kind used for deliveries. There were no windows in the back, and it looked like it had recently been off-roading, with the mud splattered halfway up the sides. If someone wanted to do something in secret, that was the place to do it.

Shane circled the block and came back. He could see no one in the van, but the front windows had an unnecessarily heavy tint on them. Everything about the vehicle seemed conspicuous.

He turned down the street next to Moran and Moran and braked almost immediately when someone ran in front of the vehicle. It took him a moment to realize that it was the ghost that typically loitered out front of the antique store.

Shane started driving again, forcing the ghost to pass through the car into the passenger seat and sit.

"You have to help Mr. Moran," the ghost insisted as Shane drove to the end of the block and parked out of sight of the conspicuous van.

"Is he still inside?" Shane asked.

"Two men with tools went in after him, but there's something with them. It chased him into the basement."

"I know about that one," Shane said. "Tell me about the men."

He got out of the car and walked halfway back up the block, tucking down the alley that ran behind James' shop. It was normally used for garbage for several businesses in the neighborhood. It led to a back door that Shane had entered once or twice before.

"Two guys came out of a van. They must have sent the thing into the basement. I've never seen anything like it."

"Are they armed?"

"What?" the ghost asked as Shane approached the rear of the antique shop.

"The men. Do they have guns?"

"Oh. I don't know. It's the ghost you should worry about; it's a monster."

"I know," Shane said. "Where are these men?"

"Mr. Moran locked himself downstairs. They're trying to break in, but the door is strong, and they weren't expecting it. Last I saw, they were still trying to get through it."

"Good. Are you helping?"

"What do you mean?" the ghost asked.

They stood in the dimly lit alley, Shane's hand on the doorknob. He couldn't hear any sounds from inside, but everything was likely muffled underground.

"Are you fighting with me?"

"Me? No! That thing—"

"Then stay out here," Shane said, cutting the ghost off. "If you can't fight, you're in the way."

The ghost almost looked offended for a moment but then nodded. Shane had rarely spoken to the spirit in the past, just a nod of greeting now and then, but he had seen it many times. He assumed he was an old friend of James', maybe even a business associate. Whatever the case, he seemed good at loitering, and he could continue to do that if he wasn't going to offer assistance.

Shane opened the door carefully and looked inside the shop. James' back door was at the end of a short hallway, and from it, Shane could neither see nor hear much of anything. He took a step inside and quietly pulled the door closed behind him.

A muffled thump made Shane stop and listen. Someone was banging on something below. A moment later came the sound of muffled voices speaking to one another, though the words were impossible to make out.

He moved silently from the back door and through the small space at the rear of the shop. James kept a storage area back there, mostly for the genuine antiques he sold, as well as a washroom, a small kitchenette, and his office. The door to the basement was open.

As Shane got closer, he could hear the voices more clearly. Two men were discussing their efforts to get past the locked door. There was very little room at the bottom of the stairs, as Shane recalled from his past visits. Nothing but a landing in front of the door big enough to stand in but little else. They would see Shane coming if he confronted them. If they were armed, he was dead.

Shane left the basement and headed to the front of the building, entering the antique shop from the main door. He opened it with as much noise as possible, letting the door chimes jingle to let the intruders know someone had entered the store.

He moved quickly behind the counter near where James kept the cash register and ducked. The spot gave him a view toward the front and rear entrances through a glass cabinet. He was hidden in shadow, and no one would see him unless they looked directly at him.

A stranger appeared from the rear of the store moments later. Shane did not recognize the face, though he only got a glimpse of a man with a mustache and stubble on his chin and cheeks. The man headed toward the front door and pushed it open, looking out onto the sidewalk before turning and looking around the shop.

The Harvester wore blue jeans, cowboy boots, and a button-down plaid shirt with tight cuffs. He didn't look prepared for a fight, but he was fairly large, and it looked like he might be able to throw a good punch if he had the chance.

"Who's there?" the Harvester asked, walking slowly among the antiques.

Shane moved silently to the end of the counter behind which he hid and waited until the man got close. Once his back was turned, Shane stood behind him, slipping an arm around the Harvester's neck while kicking out his ankle and forcing him to the ground.

The man collapsed with Shane on top of him, squeezing his neck hard and keeping his mouth covered. The Harvester struggled and Shane pulled tighter, using his free arm to brace himself.

Shane's arm was locked in place, and he applied as much pressure as he could. He held fast, and the man thrashed until his body gave out and he crumpled onto the tile floor. Shane moved with him, unwilling to let go, and flattened against his opponent's back. He couldn't hear anything, but he felt a crunch vibrate through his arms as the Harvester went limp.

The sound of something breaking down the stairs caught Shane's attention. The door must have finally given way. He took a gun from the fallen Harvester and proceeded to the rear of the store and the stairs that led to the basement.

A glance down the stairs revealed nothing. The door was open, and a handful of tools were scattered on the ground that had been used to pry and break through the door. Shane headed down as quickly as he could without making a sound.

"Lamar, you good?" someone shouted from deeper in the basement.

Shane hid behind the stairs and then peered around the corner. A man, his back to Shane, was walking down the hallway to the left. At his side was the largest Hound Shane had seen. It was leading the Harvester to the leaded glass prisons.

They were headed towards James Moran.

CHAPTER 4

DEAD TO RIGHTS

The Harvester stopped at a sealed door as the Hound continued toward the leaded cells. Shane waited as the man knelt, pulled out a flat packet of lock picks, and started working on the lock before he left the stairwell.

"Was it Goff at the door?" the man asked, hearing Shane's footsteps and thinking it was his buddy.

Shane said nothing until he was behind him.

"Nope, 'fraid not," he said, slipping an arm quickly around the front of the Harvester's face and pulling his head up as he dropped his weight onto the man's back with his knee.

The Harvester's body pressed against the door and Shane's full weight came back on his head and neck. It snapped audibly, and they fell to the floor together. Shane was up in an instant, dragging the man's corpse out of his way and then finishing the work he started with the lock picks.

When the door opened, Shane saw James sitting on a chair in the glass cage, sipping a bottle of water, and watching the Hound that watched him. The ghost sat on its haunches like a dog, and it turned its head when Shane entered, expecting to see the Harvester.

Seeing Shane for the first time, the ghost's teeth chattered together, and it stood.

"You look comfortable," Shane said to James.

"I'd rather be at home with a Scotch," the other man replied.

"Well, give me a second."

The Hound rushed him and rose on its hind legs. It was eye to eye with Shane, though there were no eyes in its sockets, and reached for him with both hands as though intent on choking him.

No one had told the creature about Shane. It had come to hunt James Moran and had no reason to believe it was in danger. When Shane caught it by the wrists as it came for him, it registered surprise on its mostly flayed face.

Shane held it steady by the wrists and kicked the ghost hard on the inside of its already disjointed left knee. Whoever had designed the Hound had made it so that its leg bent forward and backward, but it was never intended to go sideways.

Shane put as much force into the kick as he could. Since the joint and ligaments had already been broken, little was holding it together inside the ghost's body. When his boot hit ghostly flesh, the pressure tore the limb asunder, breaking the bottom half away from the thigh.

The Hound collapsed but did not give up. Hobbled on one side, it grabbed at Shane's legs and dragged him down to the floor. The lipless mouth snapped at him while the icy hands again went for his throat.

Shane kept one hand on the ghost's neck, keeping the mouth at bay, and worked the body with a series of punches. He had to avoid the ghost's ribs because they were already exposed, and he was at risk of stabbing himself on the jagged bone fragments. His only other option was punching the ghost in the stomach and soft tissue, which didn't seem to faze it.

The Hound pulled Shane close. It had a lot of upper body strength. The man who had been tortured and killed to make the spirit was in good physical condition, and that strength had carried over into death.

Shane pushed off the wall with his feet and forced the Hound into a roll. He ended up on top of the ghost and used his body weight to force its hands down and then punched it in the face.

Their roles reversed quickly as the Hound jerked and twisted its body, forcing them to roll again. They ended up face to face on their sides, and Shane clipped the Hound in the mouth with two quick left jabs, breaking loose some of its exposed teeth.

The Hound switched tactics and left Shane's neck, instead going for his eyes. The cold hands grasped his face, and he felt a thick, blunt thumb pushing into his eye socket.

Shane shook his head to pull away as he squeezed the ghost's wrist tightly. He pushed and forced it back. At the same moment, he kicked the Hound several times, hitting it in its good knee as well as landing some blows farther up on the body. The ghost barely reacted to his maneuvers.

Shane used the position they were in to his advantage and, while still holding the ghost's wrist, braced himself with his feet and then brought his legs up higher. The Hound was not used to fighting. It had no formal training and struggled dumbly as Shane hooked his right leg over the ghost's arm and locked his legs together while pulling back on the ghost's wrist.

The maneuver was quick and fluid, putting the arm in a tight leg lock while he used the leverage of his body to overextend it. The ghost's arm broke, and Shane kept pulling as hard as he could, squeezing tightly with his legs until he felt flesh tear.

The thing didn't make a sound as Shane jerked his body, digging his heels into the ghost's ribs. The Hound's lower arm pulled away from the broken elbow. An instant later, the severed appendage evaporated in Shane's hands.

Undeterred by losing an arm, the Hound twisted its body toward Shane. Its broken ribs allowed its torso to move in a more snakelike manner than any living person. It was able to nearly fold itself in half and bite Shane's shoulder before he kicked the ghost in the gut and forced it to roll away.

Hands freed up and no longer tangled with the Hound, Shane steadied himself on the floor before pulling his legs back and then kicking the ghost square in the mouth as it rolled back toward him.

More teeth broke free in its jaw, and Shane got to his feet. The Hound shook its head unsteadily and immediately jerked to the left, looking at something over Shane's shoulder.

Behind him, James had opened the door to the glass cage. He stood in the doorway, holding the glass panel in one hand, and crouched as though he might jump on the Hound.

"The hell are you doing?" Shane asked.

Before James could answer, the Hound bounded toward him. Shane tried to get a hand on the spirit, but it moved deftly, even with an arm and a leg missing. The ghost jumped and James quickly stepped aside, pulling the door toward him like a shield and leaving the doorway to the cage open.

The Hound hit the ground inside the cage and spun, bending its one good leg back and springing back the way it had come. James tried to close the door, but the ghost got its hand on the glass and forced it to stay open. They struggled briefly as the Hound eased its way out of the cage and back into the room.

Shane took hold of the door in one hand and swiped at the Hound's hand with the other, knocking it from the glass. The door swung in and slammed against the side of the monstrous thing's head. The Hound wriggled and tried to push free, keeping the door open by using its head as a wedge, but Shane simply pushed harder.

The smooth edge of the glass door pressed into the ghost's flesh. Shane put all his weight behind it and slammed as hard as he could. The door closed over the Hound's neck, separating its head from its shoulders.

The head faded from existence as though made from dust and smoke. The body inside the cage burst, but the glass absorbed the force. Shane didn't even feel a vibration through it as the door slammed shut and the lock clicked into place.

Shane collapsed to the floor, catching his breath. James stepped past him and proceeded to the doorway. Out in the hall, he began searching the pocket of the Harvester Shane had killed on the way in.

"There was a second man," James said, pulling a paper from the dead man's back pocket. "I heard them talking."

"He's upstairs," Shane said. "Won't be coming down. There's probably a third waiting in a vehicle outside, though."

"Any more of these Hounds?" James asked.

"Doubtful. No reason to send them all at once," Shane replied, hoping he was right,

He got to his feet and joined James over the corpse in the hallway. James held a slip of paper, which Shane took and glossed over. It was a receipt for a diner in Vermont from that morning. The Harvester had ordered eggs, toast, and coffee. Nothing particularly interesting, but the time and location might have relevance.

Shane put the receipt in his pocket for later.

"No identification," James said.

"I don't think these guys carry membership cards," Shane agreed.

They headed upstairs together, taking it slowly and quietly in case anyone else had come into the building. On the main floor, Shane found no sign that a third man had entered. The dead body in the shop was where he'd left it. James quickly went through that man's pockets as well but found nothing but loose change and a locked cell phone.

"I'm going to check on that van," Shane said, peering out the blinds to the dirty white van parked next to the sidewalk.

"We need to do something with these bodies," James pointed out.

"Got a dumpster?" Shane asked. "I'll be back."

He headed outside. The rear door of the van was pointed toward the antique store. With no windows, the only way for anyone inside to see him would have been to look in the side-view mirrors. Since he wasn't the target, Shane hoped that he would be ignored until he got close enough.

Shane casually made his way to the window on the passenger side of the vehicle. The tint was dark, but at such close range, he could see inside. No one was in the cab of the vehicle. If a third man was the getaway driver, he wasn't doing his job very well.

No other pedestrians were on the street, and vehicle traffic was limited. One car drove past in the opposite direction, but the driver didn't even glance. Shane doubled back to the rear of the van and put his hand on the door handle.

He thought he heard a sound from within; not a voice but someone grunting, perhaps. He waited another moment, and nothing else happened. Preparing himself for anything, Shane pulled open the door.

CHAPTER 5
DARK DEEDS

A man was laid out in the back of the van, face up, staring at the ceiling. His breathing was quick and erratic, and Shane saw blood pooled on the floor next to him.

At first, he was unsure what he was looking at, but then he realized that the blood was coming from a wound in the man's chest. The front of his shirt was torn apart, and the flesh beneath was exposed and badly damaged. A twisted piece of metal sat on the floor of the van next to him, stained with fresh blood.

"Amateur move," Shane said.

The man lifted his head at the sound of Shane's voice. He glanced at him and exhaled loudly, then groaned as his head slammed back to the floor of the van. The piece of metal looked like it might have once been a pendant of some kind. Shane could still see a chain attached to it. If he had to guess, it was probably the Hound's haunted item. The man on the floor of the van had been holding it in his breast pocket.

"Help me," the man moaned.

Shane hopped in the van and pulled the door closed. He opened the Harvester's shirt and inspected the wound.

"Come on," Shane said. "It's not that serious."

In truth, it was a deep wound. When the haunted item exploded, it looked like the man's flesh absorbed more of the blast than his pocket had. Glinting fragments were inside the exposed, bloody muscle. If the shrapnel had gone deep enough, the man could have been in danger. Shane didn't care.

He went through the wounded man's pockets and found another receipt from the Vermont diner.

"This where you guys came from? You based in Vermont?" Shane asked, showing the man the receipt.

"I need... I need a doctor," the man replied.

"You need to answer my questions," Shane countered.

"Get me to a hospital," the man insisted, struggling through the words. "Or you get nothing."

Shane smiled at the man, leaning down so they were face to face. He set a hand gently on his chest and then pressed his finger against the wound. The Harvester thrashed, gritting his teeth to hold back a scream, and stared angrily back at Shane.

"You're missing the big picture here, friend. I have all night. I don't think you do."

"You get nothing if I die," the man said, but there was no confidence in his voice.

"Then I'll be no worse than I was five minutes ago. How about you?"

The man was sweating, and Shane pressed on the wound. The Harvester gasped, and his eyes darted about as though looking for a way to free himself. He struggled, and Shane pressed the wound harder.

"Clock is ticking," he said.

"I don't know anything," the Harvester replied in between gasps. "I just go where they ask me to go."

"Who?" Shane asked.

"The Harvesters. I just drove the van."

"Who told you to come here? Give me a name."

"It was Roy. It's Roy. He said... he said we needed this guy. James Moran. We needed James Moran."

"Kidnap or kill?" Shane asked.

"Kidnap. We had to bring him back. He could be hurt but not dead."

The man struggled to get the words out, wincing as he did so. His jaw was clenched so tightly that it might as well have been locked, and his hands were balled into fists. The sweat on his eyebrows made him look like he'd run a marathon, but instead of flushed red, he was deathly pale.

Shane looked at his feet and saw that he was crouching in blood. The man was bleeding out quicker than he thought.

"Where were you going to take him?" Shane asked.

"Please," the man begged. "I need a doctor."

"Did that eyeless guy ever beg for a doctor?" Shane asked.

The Harvester shook his head, brow furrowed in confusion.

"What?"

"The Hound. The monster you brought. When you were torturing him, did he beg for a doctor before he died?"

"I never... I never did that. I just... drive."

"You don't kill them?" Shane asked.

"No. No, I swear," the man gasped.

Shane grunted.

"I don't call doctors," he replied.

The Harvester let out a pained whimper, staring at Shane. He shook his head weakly but didn't say anything else. Shane stared at him as the seconds ticked by, watching the man's eyes. When he didn't blink again, draw another breath, or make another movement, Shane turned and left the van.

He returned to the antique store, but the body that he had left there was missing. James appeared in the doorway at the rear of the shop, an iron bar in his hand until he saw it was Shane.

"The third man?" James asked.

"Dead. Blew himself up with a haunted item."

"Foolish," James said. "Anything useful on him?"

"Another diner receipt. Nothing helpful."

Shane joined James in the back and found the older man rifling through files. The corpse from the front of the store was now near the back door. The other man had been dragged to the bottom of the stairs and left there.

"I got a call from someone claiming to be Mr. Shadow before the Hound arrived," James explained.

Shane raised an eyebrow. Ghosts did not often make calls.

"Not a friendly chat?" Shane asked.

"A taunt. He mentioned the name of Ezra Deacon. He said that was where the Harvesters started."

"Ezra Deacon?"

Shane did not recognize the name, but if Shadow had said it to James, it had to have been for a reason.

"Deacon did business with Moran and Moran when I was a boy. He dealt with my father. The man's been dead for the better part of half a century as far as I know," James said.

He rifled through more paperwork from an old file box in a closet, skimming page after page.

"Did he have a beef with your old man?" Shane asked.

"I have no idea," James replied. "My father brought me into the business when I was a young man. But things that happened when I was a child were mysteries. There would have been no reason for him to include me in anything when I was still in school."

"But Shadow seems to think you know about it."

"Hard to say. Maybe he thinks one Moran is as good as another. Sins of the father and all that. Maybe he's just stark raving mad."

"There's evidence to support that theory," Shane said.

"Whatever the case, I don't know what business my father had with Deacon. He could have sold him a haunted Hummel figurine, he could have been involved in importing, or they could have been bitter enemies. I just don't know."

"Nothing in those files?" Shane asked.

James had pulled several boxes from the storage closet in his office and was leafing through them all quickly.

"The problem with my father was that he was a man of few words. He loved numbers. He kept impeccable financial records. But his notes were few and far between. There's no story here, no background information on the clients or the objects. He would make a note like 'pre-Victorian amethyst brooch. Star-shaped. Haunted by the spirit of elderly woman who speaks Russian and hates children.'"

"Efficient, if brief," Shane said, looking at the thick, blocky script on the page.

"He didn't explain where it came from, or if the ghost was dangerous. Not much of anything."

Shane volunteered to get the corpse from the basement while James went through more of his father's files in the hopes of finding something about Ezra Deacon.

He dragged the man up the stairs and placed him with the other body near the back door. They would have to bring the white van that the Harvesters had used to the rear entrance, load the two corpses into it, and then find somewhere to dump it.

Mr. Shadow probably wouldn't report the van missing, but Shane didn't want to leave it lying around where someone could notice the smell, either. Or where the police could give it a ticket.

"Ezra Deacon," James said from his office, drawing Shane's attention.

"You found something?" Shane asked, stepping into the doorway. James was standing over a new box, a sheaf of papers in his hand.

"It looks like Deacon was a regular customer of my father's in the fifties and sixties. He purchased several haunted items. Sterling silver candelabra, dented, haunted by a poet who is keen on conversation," James read. "Hunting knife, six-inch blade, bone handle, haunted by mostly faceless hunter killed by wolves. Doesn't speak, prone to violence."

"Interesting mix," Shane said.

"It goes on like that. There's a haunted soap dish, a Smith and Wesson

Model One revolver, and a straight razor. Some are the most mundane spirits; others are killers. No rhyme or reason. The sales receipts cover at least twenty-three years of business that I can see."

He kept rifling through the files while Shane glanced at the back door. He wanted to get the bodies out sooner rather than later. In his experience, the longer you left a body around, the more chances there were for someone to discover it.

"Shane," James said suddenly.

He had plucked a sheet of paper from the files and was holding it up.

"What's that?"

"Drowned man. Exceptional decomposition. Highly dangerous. There's a sketch," James said, turning the paper around.

Shane looked at the image at the bottom of the page. It was rough, but the semi-skeletal, rotten nature of the spirit's appearance was clear enough. He'd destroyed that ghost in a school while looking for Beatrix. It was one of Beatrix's prey ghosts, one that James had previously directed him to.

"That looks familiar," Shane said.

"One of my father's earlier sales. And this one," he said, turning another sheet toward Shane.

"Yeah," Shane agreed. It was the pale ghost with long, black hair that tried to suffocate him in Beatrix's old house.

"Tell me, what was the item the ghost Cassius was bound to?" James said as he set down the two pages he'd found and began looking through others.

"Straight razor. Old one, obviously," Shane said.

"Familiar?" James asked, holding up another sheet.

Shane did not read the words but focused on the sketch. It was more poorly rendered than the swamp ghost had been, but it was Cassius.

"That's him," Shane confirmed.

James put down page after page and Shane sorted them based on the sketches, looking at roughly drawn faces done in pencil half a lifetime ago or more. Some were unfamiliar to him, but some were not. The scarecrow. The unsettling spirit in the woods. The spider-like ghost that climbed the basement walls. They were all there.

"My father sold all of these to Ezra Deacon," James said.

"Half of them were at Beatrix's house," Shane pointed out.

James nodded, not bothering to look through any more of what he had.

"Deacon died, and someone—Beatrix's parents, this Mr. Shadow, or someone yet unknown—divided up his collection but did not lose it. Beatrix can be tied to every one of these."

"And they're all tied to your father. And now you," Shane said.

James didn't respond. For Mr. Shadow to bring this up, to send a Hound for James, meant there was some kind of grudge. He blamed James' father for something. What the hell had happened between him and Ezra Deacon? And how did Mr. Shadow fit in?

"I don't understand," James said.

"Which part?" Shane asked.

"Any of it. I don't understand what any of this has to do with me."

"Ghosts can carry grudges for lifetimes," Shane said. As near as he could figure, this had nothing to do with James Moran III.

But that didn't matter to Mr. Shadow.

CHAPTER 6

BODY MOVING

"It seems likely to me that Mr. Shadow is the spirit of Ezra Deacon," James said.

The thought had occurred to Shane as well, but he was not entirely convinced. Why would Deacon wait all this time to come after the son of the man who'd sold him a bunch of ghosts half a century ago? What was to be gained from starting the Harvesters, working with Beatrix, and creating the Hounds?

"Something more is going on," Shane said. He could not imagine what, but this was something bigger than Ezra Deacon and a business dispute with James' dead father.

"You said yourself that ghosts carry grudges for lifetimes," James countered.

"But why? Cassius came into Winston's possession through a fraudulent sale decades ago. Someone tricked him into buying the razor, and he kept it locked in lead all this time. If Deacon was the seller, why did he do that? Especially if he sent Beatrix to get the ghost back all these years later?"

James did not have an answer. As far as Shane was concerned, it didn't matter. Whether Mr. Shadow was Ezra Deacon or someone else, he was dangerous. He was killing people to create monsters, and he seemed to have it in for James Moran. Deacon was just a piece of information they could use. Maybe he was the start of the Harvesters.

"Do we have an address for Deacon?" Shane asked.

"He lived in Syracuse. But, as I've said, he's been dead for decades.

This address might not even exist anymore."

"I think we should find out," Shane said. "Did Deacon have family?"

"Not a clue," James said.

Shane didn't like trying to solve a puzzle with fifty-year-old pieces, but it was all they had for now. Deacon sounded like he had been a wealthy man. He had purchased several ghosts, and Shane didn't doubt that the elder Moran was not giving them away.

Even if Deacon had been dead all these years, he might have left something behind. His collection of spirits had left his possession, but Shane had never met a ghost collector that prolific who didn't have a much greater collection of non-haunted things and a large house in which to keep them. Ezra Deacon had to have left behind a legacy.

Shane looked at the bodies by the back door and nodded. They were pushing themselves into a corner, and it was a good idea to start clearing things up before they got worse.

He retrieved his phone from his pocket and scrolled to the number for Xander Ventura. It rang three times before the other man answered.

"Ryan?" Ventura said, his voice tired. Shane looked at a clock on the wall in James' office. It was late. Or early, depending on one's perspective.

"Need you to check out an address for me," Shane said.

"Do you have any idea what time it is?" Ventura replied.

"I just looked at a clock, yes. Can you find out who lives at this address?"

Ventura sighed, and Shane could hear movement in the background as the man got out of bed. Shane gave him a moment.

"Give it to me," Ventura said.

Shane took one of James' invoice forms and read the address for Ezra Deacon. He heard Ventura typing keys and then pause.

"Sydney Deacon," Ventura said. "That who you're looking for?"

"Probably."

"And you plan to go there right now?"

"I'm standing in James Moran's shop looking at two dead bodies. A third one is parked in a van out front. We need to go there right now," Shane replied.

"Jesus, Ryan. Do I want to know how those men died?"

"They died trying to kill me with a Hound and kidnap James," he said. Ventura grunted, and Shane heard more movement.

"You're going to cost me my pension," the agent said.

"Pension? How old are you?" Shane asked. Ventura was far too young to be fretting over lost pensions. He was far more likely to be arrested as a co-conspirator and face prison time.

"You cannot break into that house," Ventura said. "I just looked up that address on my computer with my government ID. I'm going with you."

"Where are you?" Shane asked. He thought Ventura might be stationed in Boston, but he'd run into him in New York once, and Vermont as well.

"I'll meet you there. I can send someone to investigate the bodies at the shop—"

"No," Shane said. "They'll be gone by the time they arrive. There was an accident at a quarry about thirty miles from here. I'll tell you where later if you want. That's where they'll be."

"You can't tell me stuff like that," Ventura complained.

"Who's telling you anything? Just saying I heard about three idiots who drove into a quarry and got themselves killed."

"Stop talking. I'll text you the address of a place in Syracuse. I'll meet you there, then we can go to Deacon's house, and you can explain at least a little of what's happening."

"I'll see you there," Shane said, hanging up.

"We're going to Syracuse, then?" James said.

It was about a four-hour drive, and it was already late, but Shane didn't want to wait until morning. There was only so much time before Mr.

Shadow realized he had failed to get James, if he didn't already know. They needed to be someplace else, somewhere harder to track.

"We are. With a slight detour along the way."

Shane took the Harvester's van and drove it to the alley behind James' shop, and the two men placed the dead men in the back. Shane destroyed their cell phones in case anyone was tracking them, and then gave James the keys.

"Just follow me. Keep it under the speed limit," he advised.

James did as instructed, following Shane in the van after stowing his files and locking the shop. If anyone came looking, they would have found nothing out of the ordinary in the store.

Shane led the way to an old granite quarry in Massachusetts that had been closed down for as long as he could remember. People swam there sometimes, but only the risk-takers, as it wasn't open to the public due to underwater hazards. A few people had died after cliff jumping and landing on some hidden granite peaks below the surface.

They pulled into the quarry in the blackness of night. The place was miles from any town, down a stretch of road that went nowhere but the quarry. It was about as isolated a place as Shane could imagine.

Shane and James lugged one of the bodies into the driver's seat and propped the man up, then did the same with another in the passenger seat.

They stopped to rest afterward, with James drinking from a bottled water he'd brought with him.

"You do this sort of thing often?" he asked, passing the bottle to Shane.

"Often? Not really," he answered, taking a drink.

"If we drive this into the quarry, the police will know these men were murdered since none of them drowned," the older man pointed out.

"Not if they hit that first," Shane said. James was giving the police a lot of credit in this situation. Shane wasn't sure anyone would even report these men missing.

He pointed to the sheer face of the rock cliff ahead of them, overlooking the edge of the water that filled the quarry below. It was a massive, flat, stone surface that would have been an ideal starting point for those looking to dive into the water. Now, it was an ideal place to drive a van into.

Shane started the van and placed the foot of the dead man in the driver's seat on the accelerator, fixing his hands to the wheel as best as he could before shifting the vehicle into drive. The door slammed as he backed away and watched the van barrel toward the wall.

The front end crunched loudly against stone and then grated across the surface to the left before tipping over the ledge and tumbling into the water. It didn't look like it had hit quite hard enough to break the necks of two men, but the fall that followed wouldn't have done anyone any favors. It would have to be good enough.

"I certainly didn't plan on disposing of any bodies today," James said.

"Most people don't until it happens." Shane shrugged.

They walked to the edge of the quarry. Light from a faint crescent moon reflected off the surface, a slash of white on black. The last few bubbles rose from where the van had sunk. By the time anyone discovered the vehicle or the bodies in it, Shane doubted there would be any physical evidence linking him or James to the victims. Assuming anyone discovered it at all.

They returned to Shane's car and headed back down the dark, dirt road that led away from the quarry. They were back on the highway in no time, heading west out of Massachusetts toward New York State.

Shane did not recognize the address they had for Deacon in Syracuse. He had only passed through the city a few times and didn't know the area well. But Ventura had provided him with the address to a restaurant where they could meet ahead of time, and he assumed the agent knew the area better than he did.

They had been on the road for nearly two hours when James turned to Shane. He looked tired.

"What if we're just showing up at Deacon's daughter's house? Or his grandchild? And they have no idea what we're doing there?" he asked.

"Won't know until we get there," Shane said.

"This is all so confusing. There was nothing unusual in my father's files. He sold Deacon haunted items, the same as he sold them to a hundred other people. The same as I sell them to people. I saw nothing untoward; nothing suspicious or more dangerous than anything else."

"People have secrets; you know that," Shane said. "You also said your father wasn't big on detailed records beyond the finances. We have no way of knowing what happened. Maybe your dad got involved in something shady. Maybe one of these ghosts killed someone important. Maybe Mr. Shadow is three bananas short of a fruit salad. You can't look for logic in these kinds of things until you know all the details. And even then, it might never make sense."

"Does that not frustrate you?" James asked.

Shane retrieved a cigarette from the pack in his pocket. He opened the window before he lit it, a small concession to the guest in his car, before answering. The window pulled the wisps of smoke from between his lips as he spoke.

"If I let every frustrating thing I encounter frustrate me, I would have gone insane years ago."

"That doesn't even make sense," James replied.

Shane inhaled from the cigarette again and glanced at his friend.

"Frustrating, isn't it?" he said.

James looked at him blankly for a moment and then, despite himself, stifled a laugh, and shook his head.

"Oh my God, Shane Ryan. I don't know how you live this life."

He sounded even more tired as he exhaled loudly, and Shane shrugged.

"This isn't a typical Thursday night for me, just so you know. I try to keep it quiet and calm whenever possible."

"So, killing three men and dumping them in a quarry after fighting off a nightmare ghost in a basement isn't typical for you?"

"That's usually just weekends."

"Of course," James said, nodding. "I'm… I don't know. I thought my days of life-threatening adventure ended when I left the service. I'm an intermediary. I have dangerous things, but I don't get involved with dangerous things. But lately, it seems like death and torment and abject horror are looming around every corner."

"Our lifestyles lend themselves to it," Shane said.

"Yes, but my father never endured this. He was never plagued by vengeful spirits. Cults never kidnapped him. Monsters never attacked him in his office."

Shane exhaled another puff of smoke and glanced at his friend.

"You sure about that?" he asked.

James returned the glance.

"What do you mean?"

"You said it yourself earlier. You were a child. Why would your father involve you in the details? Wouldn't he have kept things like this from you? Seems likely he might have had to tangle with at least one or two ugly incidents in his day, he just kept it from his family. What kind of dad would tell his kid about any of this?"

"But he didn't keep things from me. I took over the business from him."

"As a man, sure. But how old were you when these Deacon sales happened? Maybe something was there, your old man thought he'd taken care of it, years passed, and he didn't bring it up to you at all because, for him, it was dead and buried."

"Perhaps," James conceded.

The problem, Shane realized, was that in their line of work, just because something was dead and buried, didn't mean it couldn't come back.

CHAPTER 7

BLOODLINES

They arrived in Syracuse well past midnight. Ventura had given them the address of a 24-hour diner called Bugsy's. When Shane pulled into the parking lot, two other cars were there, and though he didn't think it had anything to do with the name, the two large, yellow floodlights on either side of the door had attracted a swarm of bugs that threatened to smother anyone who dared enter.

Bugsy's Diner looked like something that time had forgotten in the mid-eighties. It was a squat little building at the end of a tired-looking block of stained brick vape shops, variety stores, and a shoe repair place. It looked like the part of town people only went to if they'd lived there for decades or had discovered by accident.

"This place looks like it serves tetanus," James said as he got out of the car.

Shane laughed, putting out his cigarette. He couldn't recall James ever making a joke. It was oddly refreshing.

"As a side, I'm sure," he said. They approached the door, swatting away mosquitoes and moths, and headed inside.

Agent Ventura was the only customer. A dull, dented bell over the door rang as they entered, and a dark-haired, middle-aged woman looked through the open window from the kitchen and then came out behind the counter.

"Sit wherever you like," she said. "Start you with coffee?"

"Please," Shane said.

"A tea, if you have it," James added.

The server nodded as the two men approached Ventura in a booth that overlooked the parking lot. He had half a coffee and a piece of blueberry pie in front of him.

"I was half afraid you weren't going to show up, and I'd have to track you down," Ventura said as he shook Shane and James' hands.

"I'm not that much of a jerk, am I?" Shane asked. Ventura shrugged and took his seat again as the other two men slid behind the table on the other side.

"You look like death warmed over," he said, taking in Shane's bruises.

He had not seen Shane in person since the last beating he'd taken at the hands of Lanthimos, Beatrix, and their Hounds. It had only added layers to the injuries that had put him in the hospital before that.

"Had a rough couple of weeks," Shane said.

"No kidding. Are you sure you're up to this?"

Shane fixed him with a steady glare, and the agent threw his hands up defensively.

"Just asking. So… was the mess cleaned up?" Ventura asked.

"It was. Nothing you need to worry about," Shane said.

"It sounds like something I need to worry about."

"I doubt anyone's going to be looking for it. No one's likely to find it, either."

Ventura grunted and took another sip of coffee. Shane said nothing more, and after a moment, the agent shrugged again and then picked up his fork, eating a piece of the pie.

"Any good?" James asked about the dessert.

"Not really," Ventura said. "Canned filling. Dry crust."

"I rather like canned pie filling. Reminds me of childhood," James said.

"I feel the same about canned ravioli. It's awful, and yet, I still crave it. Is that weird?"

"Weirder than a ghost from fifty years ago sending mutilated, half-faceless custom killer spirits to kill some of us? Maybe not," Shane replied.

Ventura ate more pie, and the server arrived with Shane's coffee and James' tea.

"What can I get for you?" she asked.

"Do you have cherry pie?" James asked.

"Sure do, hon," the woman replied.

"A slice of that, please," he said.

"I'm good with coffee," Shane said. The server nodded and left, and James watched her go.

"She seemed nice," he said.

"All servers are nice," Shane said.

"Not all of them. Some lack customer service skills," James said. He was still watching her as she took the glass lid off a cake stand and retrieved his pie.

Ventura laughed quietly, drinking more coffee.

"Whatever else happened, we might have facilitated a hookup. That's got to be worth it, right?" he said.

James turned back to look at the younger man.

"I'm not hooking up, Agent Ventura."

"Of course not," he said. "You're courting or something."

Shane snorted and drank his coffee.

He had grown used to working alone, doing everything alone. When he involved other people, it rarely ended well. He had lost too much in the past by allowing others to get close. More than he cared to admit even to himself.

It had been some time since he had let himself think about Jacinta. She had been too close, and she had suffered for it. It took a long time to get to the point where he was willing to be that open with someone, and he regretted it now.

After what happened to her, he had wanted to pull away again. He wanted to rely on himself and no one else. He had Carl at the house if he needed to talk to someone, which he didn't want or need to do. Still, he told himself it was an option, to convince himself that he wasn't spiraling into a depression or destroying himself slowly from the inside.

Getting James Moran involved with the Cult of the Endless Night and the Harvesters had not been Shane's intention any more than getting Agent Ventura involved had been. But the three of them were tangled up in it now. And even though three men were dead at the bottom of a quarry, and Shane had spent the past month recovering from nearly being beaten to death more than once, the trio was joking about pie in a dingy diner in Syracuse.

In a weird way, it reminded Shane of his time in Afghanistan. Even under fire from the enemy, with death looming, they found time to joke. Sometimes, it was the only way to deal with the certainty that you weren't going to live to see the sunrise. That fear bonded you to somebody else, breeding a strange kind of absurdity. You laugh so you don't scream, and you know that the man sitting across from you feels the same way. But you still move forward. It was insane by any definition, but still, you moved forward.

"Got you an extra big slice," the server said, setting the pie in front of James. "Give me a holler if you need anything else."

She left them alone, and James made a point of not watching her leave this time.

"How is it?" Ventura asked, nodding at the pie.

James dug his fork into a dry crust that flaked apart in a thousand layered crumbs, squishing the bright, red ooze out either side. He pierced a single cherry and took it with a smattering of crust into his mouth.

"Canned filling. Dry crust," he answered. "It's good."

The agent nodded his approval before changing subjects. "So, I did some more research, and Sydney Deacon is a twenty-four-year-old graphic designer who owns three properties, one of which is the one you gave me the address for. Is she designing graphics for the Harvesters, or…?"

"Looks like she's probably the granddaughter of a man who used to own all the haunted items that Beatrix scattered across the countryside," Shane said. "All were sold by James' father to Ezra Deacon."

"Ezra Deacon. He's the man behind the curtain?"

"He's been dead longer than you or I have been alive," Shane said.

"Could still be the man behind the curtain," Ventura said.

"Could be," James agreed.

"But maybe not. Feels like there's more here. I think something went down between Deacon and Papa Moran a lifetime ago, and Mr. Shadow was playing catch-up these past few years to get ready for some kind of vengeance," Shane said.

"So, who is Mr. Shadow?" Ventura asked.

"No idea. Could be Deacon. Could be another spirit Moran sold to him. Could be literally anyone else. If he had been in the house with Beatrix and her brother thirty-odd years back, he'd been building something for a hell of a long time. How long would it take to perfect the Hounds?"

"Surely that could not have kept him occupied this whole time," James said.

Shane shook his head. It couldn't have been, but it was part of it. So was grooming Beatrix to be a weapon. So was forming the Harvesters and arming them with information and tools for hunting ghosts.

"I think the Hounds were the last piece of the puzzle," Shane said. "None of us have encountered anything like them. If Shadow had them for years, there would be rumblings if nothing else. I think this was the final move before he called checkmate."

"Checkmate in a game no one else knew they were playing," Ventura said. "What the hell does it all mean? He's been plotting to kill James since he was a kid? This is a lot of work. There are too many steps, too many moving parts."

"Exactly," Shane agreed.

There was probably a lot more than they knew about. James seemed like a tangent to Shane. Like ordering a piece of pie on the side of your coffee. It could not have been Mr. Shadow's ultimate goal, but it was something else he was looking for.

"I don't know if I should be flattered or terrified," James said.

"Probably the latter," Ventura said, turning his attention to Shane. "Listen, I don't want to piss you off or anything, Ryan, but you seriously look like a dead man. You can sit this one out, you know? We're just going to look at the house, see if there's anything there. You can't be firing on all cylinders."

"Your concern is touching," Shane said sarcastically. "And if there's anything at the house? A Hound? Mr. Shadow? You going to throw your badge at them?"

Ventura sighed and glanced at James.

"Your help is appreciated. And needed," the older man assured Shane. "I suspect Agent Ventura is just… being Agent Ventura."

"He does that," Shane agreed.

"Just trying to help," Ventura said. "I know we're not, you know, besties. But I don't want you to die when we're on a job together. The paperwork would be ridiculous."

"Toss me in a quarry," Shane told him. "It'll be fine."

"It's worked so far," James added.

He finished his pie as Shane finished his coffee. Ventura was last to set down his cup and insisted on covering the bill, leaving a generous tip on the table under his coffee cup as the three men got to their feet.

The server said good night to them as they left, and James returned the farewell. Out in the parking lot, Ventura offered to take the lead on the drive to Deacon's house. They passed almost no other vehicles on the street on the way there. Syracuse, in the wee hours, might as well have been a graveyard.

The drive from the diner to Deacon's house only took about ten minutes. They were on the eastern edge of the city, in a secluded, quiet neighborhood when they came upon a large property with a gated entrance barring them from approaching the semicircle driveway.

From the road, Shane could see that the house was a large Tudor-style building that had fallen into a state of disrepair. It didn't look abandoned or ramshackle, it just looked like someone had fired the landscapers.

The front gate was padlocked. Rust had accumulated on the chain, and Shane guessed it had probably been months since anyone had been on the property, if not longer.

"It looks empty," James said.

"Yeah," Ventura agreed. "Like I said, there are three properties registered in her name. This must just be the family house. Maybe an investment."

"Means no one will mind if we take a look around," Shane said, opening his trunk.

"I don't think it means that at all," Ventura said.

Shane returned with a pair of bolt cutters and Ventura groaned, turning his back as Shane cut the lock and pulled the chain from the gate.

"You can't commit crimes right in front of me," Ventura said.

"But I just did," Shane pointed out.

He put the bolt cutters back and pushed the gate open.

"About to trespass and break and enter, if you're curious," Shane said. Ventura shook his head.

"It was open when I drove past, and I thought I saw some suspicious activity," Ventura corrected. "After you."

Shane was the first to walk onto the property. The house laid out before him was dark, as was the rest of the property. Shade trees planted along the front wall kept most of the home out of view. On the inside, with the lack of streetlights in the neighborhood, it was hard to see anything.

It looked like a place he expected to find ghosts.

CHAPTER 8

WHAT THE PAST KEEPS HIDDEN

Shane guessed that the front door would be locked if someone had padlocked the front gate, so he didn't bother heading toward it. Instead, he circled the house, checking both the grounds and what he could see within the building as he passed windows and other entrances.

Nothing was boarded up, but every window he saw was locked. The view within was obscured by heavy drapes. At the rear of the building was a set of double glass patio doors covered only by a thin, diaphanous set of white curtains.

Shane pressed his face to the window. It was hard to see anything, but he recognized the outline of furnishings and things on the wall like framed photos or paintings. No one might live in the house, but they had left it in livable condition.

"Shane," James said, drawing his attention from the window.

Shane turned but did not need to ask what James wanted. Behind them, at the edge of the patio area before it descended into the overgrown yard, a ghost stood watching the three men.

The spirit was that of a man several inches shorter than Shane, with a receding hairline and a puffy face. He had average features and a forgettable face. He made Shane think of a bus driver or someone working a toll booth, a man you might see every day but never really look at.

"Hey," Shane said. "You wouldn't happen to know who lives here, would you?"

"No one lives there," the ghost answered. "Not in years."

"Did you know the people who did?" Shane asked.

The ghost looked from Shane to James to Ventura. The suspicion on his face was not well-masked.

"Who are you?"

"Someone who was almost murdered tonight by someone who dropped the name of the previous owner of this house," Shane answered.

"Oh," the ghost replied. He seemed to be mulling over his options.

"Just trying to put a puzzle together. Maybe not die in the process," Shane added.

"Like I said, no one's been here for years. The others come back sometimes. The same family still owns it, but they don't live here. They'll come once a year and make sure the roof hasn't collapsed, flush the toilets, check the basement, that sort of thing."

"They just leave a massive place like this unattended?" Ventura asked.

"The Deacons are very wealthy. Or they were," the ghost answered. "Mr. Deacon had many such homes once."

"Ezra Deacon?" James asked.

"Yes. That can't be who you're looking for, is it? Mr. Deacon passed many years ago, I think. It had to be… well, many."

"Did he come back?" Shane asked.

"Come back?"

"Like you. Did he come back as a spirit?"

"Oh, no. I don't think so. Not that I ever saw. I like to think I would have known about that. Maybe he did, but at another of his houses. I can't visit any of them, I'm afraid."

"Heard Deacon had a lot of ghosts once upon a time," Shane said. "A real connoisseur."

"He did," the ghost confirmed.

"Were you one of them?"

The ghost shrugged and smiled sheepishly. He turned, waving his hand toward the backyard, and then returned his focus to the three men.

"I was a gardener here once," he said. "I used to help Mr. Deacon with his ideas about landscaping back then. I showed him where certain plants would thrive, which species would complement one another, that sort of thing. You might not believe it, but there was a time when this garden was one of the most beautiful in the state. I was very proud of this once."

Shane nodded, taking in the view as best he could in the dark. It had been neglected for a long time, but there was still evidence of what it might have been back in the day. There were fruit trees, rose bushes, lilacs, and much more. The weeds had not driven everything out.

"What happened to his ghost collection?" Shane asked.

"Must have been broken up. Maybe sold off? I don't know," the ghost said. "No one told me anything. Aside from Mr. Deacon, no one else in the family could see me."

"But there's no one left in there?" Shane asked, gesturing to the house.

"I don't know," the ghost said again. "I know he kept some sealed away. Maybe they're still there?"

"Where would they be?"

"Mr. Deacon's vault in the basement. He kept all his valuable things there."

"Then we should visit the vault," Shane suggested.

The ghost looked unsure, but Shane turned his back on him and grabbed the patio door handle. The door was locked, but a well-placed kick knocked it open, forcing both doors to swing into the dark living room.

"You mind pointing out the vault?" Shane asked, looking back.

The ghost grimaced and approached, slipping into the house.

"Please don't break anything else," he asked politely.

The inside of the house smelled dusty and mothballed. It reminded Shane of untouched storage units or the way a linen closet sometimes smelled in an older person's home. It was the smell of things that had been put away and were meant to stay away.

The ghost led them down a dark hallway to a closed door that Shane opened without having to break. Ventura produced a flashlight to illuminate the steps on their way down. The basement smelled much like the upstairs, but less intensely as the cool air somewhat muted it.

Deacon's basement had a home theater in it, complete with movie theater seating and an old-school projector. There was even a home gym with workout equipment that looked like it had been transported from the sixties.

The ghost took them to a small room that was perhaps used for storage in the past but was now empty.

"Behind that wall," the ghost said, pointing at the rear of the room. There was nothing conspicuous about the wood-paneled wall.

"How do you access it?" James asked.

"Push," the ghost replied.

The room was narrow, and there was only room for two people to stand abreast inside. It was little more than a supply closet. Shane pushed the rear wall, and it depressed with a click then popped back. He took the edge and pulled to reveal a second, metal door.

The metal door was what Shane had envisioned when the ghost said vault. It was sealed tightly in its frame with a massive, heavy-looking handle underneath a combination dial. The metal of the door was dark, and the edges had rusted very slightly over the years but, for the most part, it seemed in good condition.

"You wouldn't happen to know the combination, would you?" Shane asked.

"You don't need it," Ventura said, pointing to the edge of the door with his beam of light. "Both locks are open."

Shane looked at the side of the vault door. If secured, it probably would have been as solid as a bank vault, but Ventura was right. The door was shut, but no one had locked it.

"Mr. Deacon kept haunted items in there?" James asked.

"Yes, sir, he did," the ghost replied.

"How many are still inside?"

"I wouldn't know."

"You've never looked in all this time?" Shane asked.

The ghost shrugged and approached the door. He extended his hand and then leaned against the metal.

"He made the vault from lead. I've never been able to get inside."

Shane looked back at the other two men.

"There could be anything in there," Ventura pointed out.

"Only one way to find out. You ready?" Shane asked.

Ventura nodded while James offered a shrug before nodding as well. Shane knew neither of them could do anything if something dangerous awaited, but it seemed polite to at least ask them.

"I'm just curious to see what's in there," the ghost said, smiling. He seemed like a tourist in his home, but he was not in the way, so Shane didn't care.

The door was heavier than it looked. Shane pulled, straining to make it move. The years had not been kind to the hinges, and it took a moment to get the bulky thing to give way.

As Shane pulled back using both hands, the ghost was first to poke his head into the slowly opening crack. The door was barely half open when a damp-sounding ululating cry from within preceded something hitting the door hard.

The handle slammed into Shane, and he fell back as the door swung open. A hunched-over figure leaped from the vault onto the former gardener, who cried out in surprise while Ventura focused the light on what was happening.

Shane sat up and watched as rail-thin arms the color of a fish's belly rose and fell like the blade of a windmill, tearing into the ghost and ripping away shreds of its torso.

The ghost screamed while Shane got to his feet. The spirit attacking him was a broken jumble of parts. It looked like someone had starved and tortured the living person in the harshest ways possible. Every bone looked broken, even the fingers. The pale figure bent and swayed every which way as it savaged its target.

Compound fractures were visible through multiple open wounds. The arms and legs had been snapped so severely that it looked like they were moments from falling off the ghost's body.

It was the face that drew Shane's attention, though. Even as their guide screamed his last and his body burst, knocking Shane and the others back a step, the attacking ghost raised its head to look him in the eye. Someone had skinned its face.

The similarity to the Hounds was unmistakable, but this was not a Hound. There was no precision to the face-cutting. The bone had not been polished, and the cuts were not surgical. It looked like someone had taken a pocketknife and scraped their victim's face off in a rush.

"Jesus," Ventura whispered.

He was the only one among them who had not seen one of the Hounds, and the thing before them was a much more rudimentary version. It was like someone's sloppy prototype made more horrifying due to the lack of precision or care.

The spirits Shane had tangled with were made with intention, and they were almost artistic. They had skill behind them. The thing from the vault was much more like proof of a concept that was never fully developed.

Ventura's hand trembled, and the beam of light bobbed in the proto-Hound's eyes. The ghost growled, a deeply wet and harsh sound, and leaped at the FBI agent.

Shane was on the Hound-thing the moment it moved. He tackled it below the waist, wrapping his arms around its legs and dragging it to the floor before it could reach Ventura.

The ghost wailed, a disgusting sound like someone vomiting aggressively, and it twisted its body at an impossible angle to lash out at Shane. Ragged fingernails scratched across his scalp, but he caught the ghost's other hand before it could claw at his eye.

Ventura and James backed off quickly as Shane pulled the ghost closer by the wrist and took the broken spirit by the throat with his other hand.

He aggressively slammed the ghost's head on the ground several times, to stun it enough to stop its thrashing about like a rabid beast. It warbled and screeched and fought back in such a disorganized fashion that it almost seemed like it was having a seizure.

The ghost twisted itself again, trying to escape Shane, and planted itself face-down on the ground, using its hands and feet to crawl away like an insect. Shane let it stretch itself out and then pushed his body forward until he knelt on the creature's spine.

As quickly as he could, Shane took the ghost's head in both hands and forced its face to the floor. It struggled to grab at him with broken arms and hands but could not get a reasonable grip. Shane squeezed and pushed simultaneously until he felt the head crack. A moment later, the ghost's skull caved in, and Shane sank forward before the ghost exploded and knocked him backward. A second explosion blasted simultaneously somewhere within the house.

"Are you okay?" Ventura asked, quickly coming to his side and shining the light in his face.

Shane squinted and pushed the light away from his eyes.

"Been better," he answered.

Ventura extended a hand and helped Shane to his feet.

"That was insane," the agent said. "I've never seen anything like it."

Shane glanced at James, whose expression indicated he was thinking the same thing Shane was.

"I have," he said.

This was where the Hounds had started. Deacon had been the beginning.

CHAPTER 9

OLD HAUNTS

"How long do you think that thing was down here?" Ventura asked.

"Looks like this place was abandoned after Deacon died," Shane said.

They entered the vault, a medium-sized room lined with shelves. From the light of Ventura's flashlight, Shane saw that Deacon had stored standard valuables as well as haunted items within the room.

Several jewelry boxes held items that were not haunted but were likely worth tens of thousands of dollars, though Shane was hardly a jewelry appraiser. Some were splattered with what looked like old, dried blood. There was more on the floor, the stain so old it could probably never be cleaned.

"Gold coins," James said, showing a box to the others. "Spanish. This box alone must be worth a quarter of a million dollars."

"He's got a crown over here," Ventura added, lifting something off a mannequin head. "If this is real—"

"Likely," James interrupted, looking at it. "That's Russian. Romanov, I'd wager."

"Like… the actual Romanovs?" Ventura asked.

"Only ones I know who had crown jewels," James said. "There are millions in gold and antiques in this room."

"But do you see anything haunted?" Ventura asked.

James held up a piece of twisted metal. Shane took a closer look, turning it over in his hands. It had once been a gold cigarette lighter, a very old one, but the destruction was new. The proto-Hound's haunted item.

"ED," Shane read, his finger brushing across the initials etched into the bottom of the lighter. "This was Ezra Deacon's."

"That thing was Ezra Deacon?" Ventura asked.

Shane didn't answer. He handed the broken lighter back to James. It would be very unusual for a haunted item to belong to someone other than the ghost that was bound to it. There was usually a personal connection between ghosts and haunted items. Odds were that the thing he had just destroyed had indeed been Ezra Deacon. If that was the case, the Hounds might have started with him, but it probably wasn't his idea.

"Why would his family have trapped him down here all this time?" Ventura said.

"Maybe they didn't even know about the vault," James replied.

Shane supposed it was possible. Deacon had died somewhere nearby, the lighter was bound to him, it was in the vault, and his ghost became trapped. But he had died as that thing. That would surely have been a detail that captured the attention of law enforcement and the media. But neither Ventura nor James had come across anything about it, and that meant no one knew. Or, at least, no one had told anyone. Would a family do that?

"There are more broken things here," Shane pointed out as he approached a new shelf.

None of the items looked as valuable as the lighter. There was a pistol, a pocket watch, a human hand, and something metal Shane could not identify. Each one was badly damaged. Their ghosts had been destroyed, and Deacon had kept the broken remains, the same way Beatrix had done.

"I have files here," James said, opening a drawer and leafing through some folders.

"Anything labeled 'Hounds' or 'Evil Plans'?" Shane asked.

Shane kept looking around while James picked through papers. He saw only a handful of broken items, but there were also many boxes. Several felt lightweight, but others were heavy and lead-lined, though all of those were open and empty. There was a potential for more ghosts in the room, but he couldn't confirm anything.

"Cassius Maclay. Born nineteen-twelve in Hoboken, New Jersey," James said suddenly, reading from one of the sheets. "Fifteen murders confirmed, twelve more suspected. Claimed forty-seven but unverified and, in some cases, demonstrably false."

"He's got biographies?" Shane asked.

"Extensive," James continued, flipping to a second sheet. "Confirmation that Benedict Winston received the razor."

He flipped the sheet again and pulled up a small receipt clipped to the main package.

"It's a courier receipt," James said. "He sent Cassius to Winston via courier and kept the handwritten receipt."

"Nothing wrong with good record-keeping," Ventura said.

"Winston's smug demeanor refuses to be tamed," James continued. "He's vexatious, and his salt-of-the-earth attitude is a parlor trick for the soft-pated dunderheads who praise the likes of Jameson and Flanders at their pedestrian holiday affairs."

"Who the hell are Jameson and Flanders?" Shane asked.

James shrugged and kept reading.

"All he had to do was apologize, but he refuses to do so. I will show him how far his attitude gets him in the real world. Cassius Maclay will suit him well. I hope he dies screaming."

"Nice guy," Ventura said.

"So, Deacon had a grudge against Winston and sent him Cassius' razor with the intent to kill him when Winston thought he'd bought another spirit."

"But Winston kept him locked up," James finished.

"Sounds like he hated Jameson and Flanders as well," Ventura added.

James looked through more folders and pulled out another piece of paper.

"Jameson died in the morning of Saturday last. I received word from Wincott at the club. They found him in the bay. The working theory is that a shark attacked him. It was hard not to laugh. I covered by pretending to get choked up. I'm going to have lobster at Voisin tonight."

He looked at Ventura and Shane and held up more papers.

"There are dozens of these."

"He was killing people with ghosts. Anyone he had a grudge against," Shane said.

"Someone must have gotten wise," Ventura said. "Whoever's running the Harvesters now. They made Deacon their first Hound."

"Shadow," Shane said. "We're missing a step here. What connects Shadow and Deacon? And where does Beatrix come in?"

James kept pouring through the papers, shaking his head slowly.

"He sent a ghost after a neighbor who cut him off in traffic. This one was for buying a boat he wanted. Another for not inviting him to a dinner party. Some don't even have reasons," he said, reading from one sheet to the next.

"Did they all die?" Ventura asked.

"Some have details, some don't. He never mentions Winston surviving. But he talks about the neighbor's heart attack. They're put together like a business ledger but written like a madman's journal."

"Mr. Shadow had to be someone once," Shane said. "If Deacon kept thorough records, he could be in there but under his real name."

"Talbot," James said.

"I don't think so. Shadow was part of Talbot's household," Shane reminded him.

"No. Talbot," James said again, holding up a new sheet. "There are pages here. He hated him."

Shane approached for a closer look, and James handed him the first couple of pages.

"Talbot refuses to sell. I've warned him more than once. I've told him what he risks, and he laughed at me. Sometimes, I think I should save the hassle and simply shoot the man. Three spirits wasted on him already, trapped now at his Rhode Island home. I don't know how he overcomes them. I was certain Spider would succeed, and yet, nothing. Talbot was back at his office on Monday," Shane read.

"Spider?" Ventura said.

"I met him. Unpleasant, but he seemed to be a fixture. He was in your files," Shane said to James.

"He was. These ghosts are being passed around a small group. A snake eating its tail. And, it seems, doing so with the intent of killing," the older man declared.

"This seems like a real bonanza of information, but what does it mean? Deacon was a serial killer with untraceable weapons and then… he killed the wrong guy? Or tried to? They fought back, hard, and he spent half a century as a monster in his vault while his killer built a team of ghost hunters and no-faced freaks?" Ventura mused.

"Deacon was not a man who thought rationally, I'm learning," James said, looking through more folders. "We might never fully understand what he did or why."

He was about to say more but stopped short as he flipped to a new folder. They could already see the name on top, written in Deacon's oddly scratchy hand. It read "MORAN".

"Your father?" Ventura asked.

James did not answer. Instead, he opened the folder and took out a single sheet of paper.

"Moran has cheated me for the last time. He'll be repaid tenfold," James read. There was nothing else written. "Based on the date, this is the last thing he wrote."

"No explanation of what cheat he was talking about?" Ventura asked.

"Nothing. Nor the planned payback."

James continued to inspect the files while Shane returned to the shelves to see what else he could find. Not far from where some of the destroyed haunted items were sat a box, about half the size of a ring box but held closed with small clasps on three sides.

The weight of it meant it had to be lined with lead, but Shane was not keen on opening it to find out what it was. He was about to place it back on the shelf when something thumped on the floor above their heads.

Shane moved to the vault door while James and Ventura put down what they had been looking at.

"Someone is here," Shane said, hearing voices somewhere in the house.

Lights came in, not just in the vault but throughout the basement. Footsteps on the stairs indicated more than one person.

Shane dropped the small box into his pocket and ushered the other two men out of the vault. They had reached the entrance to the closet with its hidden door when a police officer appeared at the end of the hall, his gun drawn.

"Syracuse police! Let me see your hands," the man shouted. Shane cursed and slowly lifted his hands. "Into the hallway."

Shane did as instructed, just as a second officer joined the first. Behind them, Shane saw a woman in a hoodie and jeans who wasn't a police officer.

"Agent Xander Ventura. I'm with the FBI," Ventura said, entering the hallway with his hands up and his ID open for the police to see. He glanced at Shane, tight-lipped and annoyed, but proceeded slowly toward the officers.

"That's far enough," the second cop said. Ventura stopped and shook the ID still in his hand.

"Make it quick, guys; my arms are getting tired."

The first cop approached, keeping his gun trained on Ventura while his partner covered Shane. James was still in the closet, unsure how to proceed. Shane shrugged.

The police officer took Ventura's ID and looked it over, then used his radio to call in Ventura's credentials.

"Can I put my hands down?" Shane asked.

"You can shut up," the police officer covering him said.

"Why is there an FBI agent in my house?" the woman in the hoodie asked from behind the group. "Who the hell gave you permission to be here?"

"Following a lead on a case, ma'am. Saw someone break in and pursued the suspect."

The radio dispatcher called back quickly, confirming Ventura's identity and credentials. The officer grunted and holstered his gun before returning Ventura's ID.

The agent lowered his hands and Shane, despite still being covered by the second cop, did the same.

"Time's a wasting here, we're on a clock," Shane said as Ventura started explaining their presence to the first officer. His partner was still not sold, especially as James joined them in the hall.

"You're telling me you're a federal agent, too?" the officer asked, approaching Shane and James.

"Never said that," Shane replied.

"They are working with me on my case, officer. We're also on a deadline, so if we're done here…"

"Where's the suspect?" the second officer asked.

"Fled the scene," Ventura answered without missing a beat. "Wanted for questioning in several homicides across state lines as well as an arson investigation."

"We didn't get a head's up," the same officer countered.

"No, you didn't. And you won't until I need the help of Syracuse PD. Now put your weapon away; I need to finish my job."

CHAPTER 10
GRUDGES

"The ID is legit, Cabot," the other cop said.

"Doesn't mean he can just break into people's houses," Officer Cabot replied. "With, what, your poker buddies?"

Ventura took out a notebook and started writing something. The first officer looked from him to his partner and back. Cabot reluctantly holstered his weapon as Ventura took control of the scene.

"Why are you writing down his name?" the officer asked.

"No reason," Ventura replied. "Why don't we talk outside, get out of Miss...?"

"Deacon," the woman said as Ventura made eye contact with her.

"Miss Deacon's home and let her assess the damage."

The officer allowed Ventura to usher him to the stairs. James and Shane began to follow, and the other officer stopped them.

"You two have names?" he asked.

"Shane Ryan and James Moran," Ventura said without looking back. "You're holding up my investigation, Officer Cabot."

Cabot's confidence had begun to fade as Ventura's increased. The doubt that he was in the right was plain on his face, but he was also annoyed. He followed the other men out, and Miss Deacon took only a moment to investigate the vault before following as well.

"Did he say your name was James Moran?" she asked, catching up with them near the back door that Shane had kicked in. Ventura had wrangled both police officers and was talking to them very quickly, rattling off details of the crimes Beatrix and Cassius had committed when Shane first alerted him to the Harvesters.

James stopped short of joining the others on the back patio area and smiled at the young woman, nodding.

"Yes. James Moran III," he said, extending his hand.

The woman looked at it nervously for a moment. She had been under the assumption Moran was a burglar not five minutes earlier, but shook it, anyway.

"Sydney Deacon," she replied.

Sydney was older than Shane had thought at first, but not by much. Surely no older than twenty-five. Her dark hair was slightly disheveled, and her general appearance made him think she had gone to the property very hastily. They must have tripped a silent alarm that woke her wherever she had been.

"Do you sell antiques, Mr. Moran?" Sydney asked.

"I do," he said, glancing at Shane.

Sydney smiled, an awkward, self-conscious expression.

"I'm sorry. My grandfather owned this house, and he used to do business with Moran and Moran. Is one of them you? You don't look quite old enough…"

"Family business," James said. "I inherited it from my father, and he from his. We have been in antiques for quite a while."

"Legacy, yeah," Sydney said with a nod. "I understand that."

She looked at the police with Ventura, and then at James once more as she lowered her voice.

"So, as an antiques dealer, do you often break into homes with the FBI?"

"I don't make it a habit," he replied, giving her little information to work with.

"It's just that I inherited this place. It belonged to my grandfather and then my father. He passed away about three years ago, and this is just one more thing I never had time for. Big, ugly, old house full of junk no one has touched since before I was born. But I've been trying to go through everything, learn what kind of man my grandfather was, and I remember your name popping up. Your family name, at least."

She spoke as though she were trying to draw information from James. Shane listened like he was just a stranger minding his business, while Ventura handled the cops.

"I'm not fully aware of all the business our families conducted, I'm afraid," James told her, which was at least partially true.

"From what I saw, my grandfather sued your father. He never mentioned being sued?"

"No," James said, and Shane could see that was true. Moran's father was a man who kept his business to himself, even when he gave the business to his son.

"That's a shame," Sydney continued. She looked at the police again and lowered her head, speaking even more softly. "It was a weird lawsuit."

"Perhaps we can walk around to the front of the house and discuss it?" James asked.

He invited her to head that way and followed at her side. Shane joined without invitation, staying on James' other side so as to not crowd the girl. The police officers watched them go, but Ventura kept them wrapped up in the details of his investigation. It sounded like he had convinced them he was enlisting their aid.

"What made this lawsuit weird?" Shane asked.

Sydney looked at him, and for a moment, he thought she might clam up. Shane was the only member of the group who no one had identified yet, but she seemed to accept he was just part of the team.

"Well, it never came to fruition," Sydney said. "I went through all my grandfather's legal stuff first, just to see where I stood with the inheritance. A lot of boring stuff, but the lawsuit was dropped on the advice of his lawyers. He claimed in the filing that Moran and Moran had defrauded him out of…"

She looked at James and Shane again and smiled awkwardly.

"Ghosts. There's no non-crazy way to say it. He was suing over ghosts. His lawyers didn't want it to go anywhere, because obviously, right? My grandfather wasn't a politician or a super-important businessman, but people knew him. He had money and some local notoriety. It would have made him look like he had lost his mind. So, they dropped it."

"Probably a good thing," Shane said.

"Don't get me wrong, from everything I've read, my grandfather wasn't a well man at the end of his life. But, I mean, here you are all these years later. What was going on between our families?" she asked James.

"I wish I had an answer for you," he told her. "My father was not forthcoming with any of this sort of information, either."

"But then why are you here? Why now? From every story my parents told me, my grandfather was, to put it mildly, out of his mind. He had better days and worse days, but he was always weird. They won't even tell me how he died. The records are all missing. I don't know the cause, the date, the location... nothing. So, it weirds me out when this name from the past breaks into my dead grandfather's house, and people still can't tell me anything."

James sighed heavily as they walked down the semicircle driveway toward the gate. Shane could tell Moran would tell her more than she needed to know, but he didn't disagree with it. She likely knew something she wasn't letting on, too. Either they kept her in the dark and moved on with trying to find Mr. Shadow, or they took a chance on her knowing more.

"I came here because I got a phone call," James told her. "Someone told me that, many years ago, your grandfather was involved in something that has involved me in the present."

"That's very vague," Sydney said.

Shane had pulled a cigarette from his pocket and placed it between his lips. His lighter clinked softly as he flipped the lid and lit it.

"Someone tried to kill him tonight. And me, a few days back," Shane explained.

The bruises on his face were as prominent as ever, even in the poor light. She would have noticed that he looked half-dead when she first saw him in the basement.

"Someone my grandfather knew?" she asked.

"Someone who dropped his name," Shane explained. "Said he started whatever is still happening. Whoever is around today has a real grudge against us, and it looks like your grandfather was the king of grudges. As we now know, he had a beef with James' family. So maybe this anonymous call wasn't just blowing smoke."

Shane exhaled a puff of smoke to accentuate the point. Sydney looked about as confused as Shane expected.

"And you? What's your story? There's no way you're FBI. You don't look like you sell antiques, either."

"I just try to fix problems," Shane said.

"Looks like you're not batting a thousand," she told him.

"Sometimes, they're big problems."

"Nothing I know about my grandfather makes sense. I never met him; he died so long before I was born. I've only seen two photos of him. My dad never talked about him. The lawyers can't tell me anything, and all his files are so... crazy. I just want to know what's going on."

"Same boat," Shane said.

Sydney sighed, and her lips tightened. Shane could see her hands clench, and she was struggling with how to proceed.

"Does this have anything to do with Brandy Jean Talbot?" she asked, speaking very quickly as though forcing herself to even ask the question.

Shane glanced at James and then back at the young woman.

"Now *that* is a name I recognize," he said.

Beatrix's real name, as far as Shane could tell, was Brandy Jean Talbot. She had dropped off the grid and become Beatrix some years earlier.

"You know her?" Sydney asked.

Shane gestured to his face.

"A lot of this is courtesy of her," he said.

Sydney looked horrified.

"Oh, my God. She attacked you?"

"She's a quirky gal," Shane agreed. She was also dead, but he kept that to himself for now.

"I never... she's been here before. A lot. That's why I had the silent alarms installed. I thought you were her. She's broken into this house a dozen times. I keep getting restraining orders and calling the cops, but nothing sticks. She vanishes or they let her out for reasons they can't explain. She's stolen I don't know how many things from the house. I never knew she was violent, though."

"What did she steal?" James asked.

"More like, what *didn't* she steal? A watch, an urn, an old hunting knife, a pair of glasses. One thing at a time; it never makes sense. Never anything valuable. Not that there's anything of value left in the house."

"Other than the vault. She must not have found that," James said.

Shane stared at James, who realized his mistake a beat later.

"What vault?" Sydney asked.

The color drained from James' face as he kept his demeanor as casual as it had been. The cat was already out of the bag, however. Besides, Shane thought the girl could use a break.

"Your grandfather had a hidden vault at the back of that closet down there. You never knew?" Shane asked.

"No," she said bluntly. "My father never said anything like that. What's in it?"

"You'll want to take a look. I would suggest that, if you find any heavy boxes that are locked, you leave them locked."

"Why would I do that? What's in the boxes?"

Shane pulled the cigarette from between his lips, pondering the best way to address that.

"Your grandfather details a lot of his grudges in his files. You can read them down there. He sent packages to people. Things meant to hurt others, even kill them. I don't think every sealed box is safe to open," he explained.

He was either keeping the woman safe or offering her a lure she'd never be able to resist. He hoped she trusted his word. There might not have been any dangerous spirits down there. Shane had one small, lead-lined box in his pocket, but he hadn't confirmed any others were there.

"Is that what Brandy Jean keeps looking for?" Sydney asked.

"Hard to say," Shane said. "You might have noticed she's not very easy to work with."

"My grandfather had business with her father. At least somebody named Talbot. I found that in his records, as well."

"Do you know the nature of the business?" James asked.

Sydney shook her head.

"I saw some invoices, but they were for lot numbers, no specifics. My grandfather bought things from Talbot, but I don't know what. I always figured that woman was looking to steal things back, but she'd never explain what she wanted."

The information they found in the basement didn't shed much light on the nature of the deals between Deacon and Talbot, either. It was clear enough that, after their falling out, Deacon had tried to sabotage Talbot by sending him ghosts, it had just never worked out.

Ventura and the police officers approached the trio from the rear of the house. Officer Cabot passed without a word and went to the car while Ventura shook the hand of the other officer and wished him well.

"Miss Deacon, I'm sorry for the inconvenience," Ventura said after the cops had left, then handed her a card. "Please call that number if you have any information regarding who might have broken in tonight."

"It was you guys," she said to him.

Ventura's smile froze on his face, and he redirected his attention to Shane.

"We might have looped her in a little. Her grandfather sued James' father once. And Beatrix has broken in here more than once looking to steal things," Shane said.

"I see," Ventura said.

"If I find out anything else about your father or this Talbot person, I'll let you know." Sydney looked from James to Shane and Ventura. "Should I be worried about Brandy Jean?"

"No," Shane told her. "I don't think she'll be back again."

They wished the woman a good night and headed off the property back to their vehicles.

"I can't be breaking and entering like this again," Ventura said once they were out of earshot. "I just sold the biggest load-of-crap story in my life to those two cops. There's no way this doesn't come back on me."

"You're not technically lying," Shane said. "This is about the murders Cassius committed. And more. There's an arson in Rhode Island you can add if you want."

"*Your* arson," Ventura pointed out.

"Of course don't tell anyone that part."

"Let's go back to the diner. I need to make some phone calls," Ventura said, getting into his vehicle.

Shane and James got into Shane's car and followed him out, while Sydney Deacon watched them all from the end of the driveway of her grandfather's house.

Chapter 11
Digging Up the Dead

James was eating his second piece of pie of the night. He had opted for blueberry this time rather than the cherry he had before. The server was delighted to see them again, indicating just how slow her night had been. The fact that they had left her a generous tip previously probably also helped.

"Okay," Ventura said, putting down his phone. He'd been talking to someone for close to fifteen minutes. "I've tracked down Mr. and Mrs. Talbot. They're in Tiverton, Rhode Island."

"Hope not in the house on the beach," Shane pointed out.

"Hillside Cemetery," Ventura said. "Been dead for years."

James looked at his watch and sighed.

"I was looking forward to a good night's sleep tonight," he said.

"You can sleep in the car," Shane said. They were looking at a solid five-hour drive, depending on how willing Ventura was to speed across three states.

"I said 'good'," James said.

"Look on the bright side: This could be a wasted trip if no one's there," Shane said.

"Isn't there always a ghost or two in a cemetery?" Ventura asked.

Ideally one or both Talbots would be haunting the place, but in a pinch, a ghostly neighbor could have some information to share.

"No," Shane said. "Always a gamble. But Tiverton had its share of the dead. If nothing else, we can head by the house again. There might be someone left there. I was more concerned with Shadow and Beatrix last time. The Talbots might be easier to track in their hometown."

"This is exhausting," James said. "I prefer dealing with living clients in search of bone China."

"Just wait until someone seriously tries to kill us," Shane said.

"Were the previous attempts on my life not serious?"

"Not really," Shane said. "You're not even bleeding. You'll know when it gets serious."

"Truly comforting," James said, finishing his coffee.

The server approached one last time as the three prepared to leave. She put the bill in front of James, though Ventura paid it. The woman tapped another piece of paper while looking James in the eye.

"Hope to see you soon," she said before walking away.

Ventura picked up the slip of paper after leaving money on the table and then handed it to Shane.

"Jeanette," Shane said, turning it to face James. She had written her phone number on it.

James' eyes widened, and Shane gave him the paper before getting out of the booth. He folded it neatly and placed it in his wallet as they walked out, smiling at Jeanette as she gave them a friendly wave.

"This is for me, you think?" James asked as they returned to the car.

"I'm upgrading you to detective," Ventura joked. "Keen investigative skills."

"Now you need to make sure you don't get killed," Shane said. "You don't want to leave her hanging."

They got into their cars, but Shane pulled out of the lot first, forcing Ventura to follow behind him as they drove out of Syracuse. He planned to set the pace a little more intensely than he figured the agent would.

James pulled out the slip of paper within five minutes, reading it over to himself before showing it to Shane.

"Her home number, you think?" he asked.

"How old are you?" Shane asked back, glancing at him. He already knew the answer, but James Moran sometimes seemed quite a bit older than his years. Must have come from spending so much time around antiques. They were rubbing off on him.

"Of course," he said. "Home number."

"No one has a home phone anymore," Shane said. "Except you. Probably Ventura. That's her cellphone. She's asking you to call her. For a date. Trip to the sock hop or an ice cream social."

"I'm not that much older than you," James said. "But I admit I have not been in a relationship in a very long time. My work doesn't lend itself to having companionship. The danger—"

He stopped, looking at Shane as an awkward realization dawned on him.

"I'm sorry, that was thoughtless."

"It's fine," Shane said. "You're not wrong. It can be hard if the two things cross at the wrong time. Very hard."

"It's likely best to just ignore it," he said, staring at the number in his hand.

"Don't ignore it," Shane advised. "Doesn't have to be serious. Life-threatening. Could be just you and that woman having a coffee or playing… you know… pinochle. It's worth it."

"Pinochle," James repeated, nodding slowly. "You know me so well."

Neither of them said anything for a long moment. They drove down a dark highway, the lights of oncoming cars occasionally flashing across their faces. Shane stared at the road ahead.

"Everyone has their time," Shane said. "Tomorrow, or thirty years from now. But when it's up, you have no idea what comes after. You might end up stuck on the side of the highway for a hundred years or more. Alone, unseen by anyone, unable to leave. So, take the time when you have it, James. Do something with it."

James did not reply. Instead, he folded the paper with the woman's phone number into a tidy little square and returned it to his wallet.

It was approaching dawn when they finally reached Tiverton. The sky was just beginning to turn from black to gray and they made their way to the small, isolated cemetery where Beatrix's parents were buried.

Shane got out of the car and had a cigarette while he and James waited for Ventura to catch up. When the agent arrived, the three entered the cemetery together.

Hillside Cemetery was one of Rhode Island's historical cemeteries that were scattered across the state. Some of them were simply family plots that had existed since before America was even a country. Many only had three or four graves. Hillside was larger, with several hundred plots. Several spirits walking among them, some clearly dating back two hundred years or more.

"Any idea where to start?" James asked.

"Let's ask a local," Shane suggested, heading for the nearest ghost.

Barely a stone's throw from the cemetery entrance was the ghost of a short man with a bent back. He had lanky arms but a pot belly and only a faint smattering of hair on his head. He looked sickly like he had waged a long battle against a disease that had eventually won, and his eyes were sunken and jaundiced.

Shane approached the spirit which, at first, paid the three living men no mind. Ghosts in cemeteries typically ignored the living as they were routine visitors and could generally be counted on to be there for the same reason every time.

It wasn't until Shane was within a few paces of the ghost that he finally looked him in the eye and realized Shane could see him. Shane was used to that awkward moment. Sometimes it was only a heartbeat, during which time he had to judge whether the ghost was going to be receptive to him or if it would react violently.

The hunched-over old man made a face but straightened up as best he could, still falling quite short of being able to look Shane directly in the eye.

"You look like you've been here a while. Think you could help me find someone?" Shane asked.

"Names are on the stones," the ghost replied sourly.

"Yes, I've noticed," Shane said. "Do you know where the Talbots are located?"

The ghost grumbled something. A few other nearby spirits watched the interaction now that they were aware Shane could see them.

"It's important we find them swiftly," James added.

"Oh, it's important," the ghost said with obvious sarcasm. "I'd hate to hold you fellows up."

Shane considered verbally sparring with the cantankerous old thing a while longer, but he had been driving all night and was not in the mood. Instead, he turned away from the ghost and headed toward the next closest one.

"Wait, now. You're going the wrong way," the ghost protested.

Shane paused and looked back at the surly spirit.

"That's where you need to go. Near the eastern fence," the ghost said, gesturing furtively to their right.

"Eastern fence," Shane said.

"Near the northeast corner. You'll see."

"Thanks," Shane said, making the course correction and heading northeast. James and Ventura followed suit.

"All you have to do is ask the right questions," the ghost called out after them. "I can be helpful."

He kept grumbling as the three men left him behind. Hillside was a sparsely filled plot of land with a lot of trees and, as the name suggested, several hills that gave the landscape character. By the time they reached the eastern fence line, they had seen at least a dozen roaming spirits.

"I don't often go to cemeteries," Ventura said, looking at the ghost of a woman in a long, black dress whose face was covered by a veil. "Scared the hell out of me as a kid."

"I don't make a habit of it, either," James agreed.

"Great place for information," Shane countered. "Just not usually very up-to-date stuff."

"When I was a kid, there was a cemetery a few blocks over. There was a ghost there that would sometimes wander through my neighborhood. I used to watch her from my bedroom window at night," Ventura said. "I told my parents about her, and they didn't believe me, of course. No one ever did."

"They usually don't," Shane grunted.

"My father could see them, too. Almost everyone in my family could. Made it a little easier to deal with," James said.

"What happened with your ghost?" Shane asked as they followed the fence, looking at the names on stones in search of the Talbots.

"She saw me one day. Really saw me. We locked eyes, and she knew that I knew, not like all the people who would walk past her and be oblivious. And she came toward the house, and it must have been the exact right distance from where she was buried. She could only just reach the wall. She could reach it and climb the outside and stand in my bedroom wall, only half in my room like she had been accidentally built into the drywall. And she watched me."

"Did she ever speak to you?" James asked.

"Yeah," Ventura said. "She'd whisper. When it was late and my parents were asleep, she'd show up and tell me to come to her."

"Did you ever approach?"

"She wanted me to come to her so she could kill me," Ventura said, "so no. I never tried it."

"She was lying, right?" Shane asked. He saw a spirit ahead, and the end of the fence as well.

"What do you mean?" Ventura asked.

"If she could reach your room, she could reach the front door, right? The lawn? The sidewalk. She ever try to kill you out front?"

"Oh. No." Ventura said. "I looked for her outside all the time. She only ever appeared in my room. And later, I saw that she was from the cemetery. I remember driving past with my parents and nearly having a panic attack when I saw her."

"So, she lied. She could have killed you coming home from little FBI school. She just wanted to scare you, get your attention. Maybe do something for her."

"Lots of better ways to ask for help," Ventura pointed out.

"There are. It's possible she just wasn't very smart, I suppose, and never thought about killing you elsewhere," Shane said.

"Point is, I never liked cemeteries much since then," Ventura concluded. "Ghosts that come to your house and threaten murder every day when you're seven years old can make you feel uncomfortable that way."

"I can only imagine," James said. Shane said nothing. The spirit ahead stood over a grave marked Talbot.

"Think we found what we're looking for," he said, changing the subject.

The ghost turned its head as they approached.

CHAPTER 12

MOTHER

The ghost was that of a woman in her forties. She had been pretty once, Shane thought, before whatever had happened to her. Her hair was a little messy, but more significantly, someone had broken her neck violently. Her head sat crookedly atop her shoulders with a bone bulging out the side. Her right eye was bloodshot, and bruising covered her from her shoulder to her hairline.

"Is that yours?" Shane asked, looking at the stone that bore the name Talbot. There were two, side by side. Melissa Rose Talbot and Lucas Talbot. They'd died on the same day almost thirty-five years ago.

"Who are you?" the ghost asked instead of answering.

"My name is Shane. I'm looking into some business your husband had with a man named Ezra Deacon."

The ghost scoffed and rolled her eyes.

"Jesus, that man. Dead for years, and I still can't get away."

"Deacon? Or your husband?" Ventura asked.

Melissa looked at Ventura, then James, assessing the three of them before continuing.

"Both, I suppose," she answered. "If you want to speak to Lucas, you're going to need a miracle. He never came back. All his years of talk, all his obsession over the afterlife and the spirit realm for nothing. He died. The end."

"Were you aware of the work he did with Ezra Deacon?" James asked.

"Work? He never worked with him. They might have claimed to be partners, but those men hated each other. I think half of what motivated anything they did was spite. One-upmanship."

"How did they know each other? What work were they doing?" Shane asked.

"Importing," Melissa answered. "Years ago, before our children were even born."

"Importing what?" Ventura asked.

Mrs. Talbot looked at him in a considering way and then glanced at the other two men again.

"Why are you gentlemen here?" she asked.

"Someone tried to kill me yesterday and said it had to do with Ezra Deacon. That led us to your husband. All of this had something to do with my father, but it was years ago when I was just a boy. I'm just trying to find out what happened," James answered.

"Ezra didn't return, did he?" Melissa said, her voice low. "He didn't find a way back?"

Shane shrugged noncommittally.

"It looks like he did, but he's not behind the threat to his life." He nodded toward James. "And he's gone again, anyway."

"Gone?" Melissa asked.

"Not everyone who comes back stays."

"I'm sorry if you're caught up in something, sir," Melissa said to James. "Something my husband had a hand in. They used to import antiques, things of 'rare cultural value', as my husband used to say. I think they were all stolen, and I think too many of them were home to dark things. Ghosts and monsters and curses galore. It's what set them at each other's throats. They always fought over money and possession and plans."

"Your husband and Deacon?" Shane asked.

"They were worse than children. Lucas would say the sky was red if Ezra said it was green, and it would still be blue the whole time."

"We understood that something happened that ended their business and made them enemies," James said.

"Yes, there was something," she said. "Lucas never explained that to me beyond accusations of theft. Mostly, he just said that it was over, and Ezra was out of our lives forever."

"How long were you free?" Shane asked.

The ghost looked at him and did a good job of keeping her expression even. But not a great job.

"Not as long as I would have liked," she whispered.

"Did your husband kill Ezra Deacon?" Ventura asked.

Melissa laughed, a sarcastic sound.

"God. I wish he had. I wish *I* had. Lucas didn't have the guts for something like that; he wasn't a killer. He was barely a conman at the best of times. Mostly, he was just a fool. A man with a hundred pounds of confidence but only a five-pound sack in which to carry it."

"What happened at the house on the beach?" Shane asked, trying to steer the ghost toward useful. If she didn't have details of her husband's business, it would be a dead end trying to focus on it. But the house and the children were something she had to know about.

"Why do you want to know about the house?" she asked, her tone becoming flat.

"Because it's haunted. And your children were there."

Shane let the blunt statement hold its own for a moment. Melissa Talbot's eyes tightened at the corners.

"My children have nothing to do with Ezra Deacon," she said.

"I think they did," Shane countered. "I met Ben there. And the host of dead things that surrounded him. And I met Brandy Jean."

"Ezra Deacon died long before they were born," she replied.

"But something your husband and Deacon did was not dead by the time those kids were born. Or by the time you died. What am I missing, Mrs. Talbot?"

The pale early-morning light seemed to catch Melissa's eyes. They looked like they were holding back tears. She shook her head, the broken neck making it a difficult gesture.

"I don't want to talk about the children."

"They died, Melissa. Both of them," Shane said.

"That's not true," the ghost said, shaking her head vigorously. "Brandy Jean got away. I heard she got away—"

"Got away from what? What happened to your family?"

"He said they'd be okay," the ghost said, straining to form the words. "He said a friend was watching the twins, and we needed to go right away. It would just be for a day or two. I didn't want to leave, but he was adamant. He forced me to go and promised they'd be okay. He swore to me."

She sobbed as she spoke, her voice filled with sadness and anger. Her husband had betrayed her in the end.

"Why did you have to leave?" James asked.

"Something happened in the house. I was never as sensitive to everything the way Lucas was. I didn't see ghosts everywhere, but I felt it when it happened. Something dark in the house. But he said I didn't understand. He said, if anything, the children would be safer without us there. He said someone was after him for what he'd done, and he just needed to get away. Not far, just a mile or two. So, we went to a hotel in town. I told myself it'd be okay since we were still so close," she said.

She paused then, staring at her husband's grave. Shane glanced at James and Ventura then returned his focus to the dead woman.

"Did you ever get home?" he asked.

"No," she said softly. "I heard later, when people at the cemetery were talking, that Ben had died. They said that Brandy Jean was missing. I never heard anything about her again until just now."

"You said your husband had done something. Did he tell you what he did?" Ventura asked. "What made someone come after him?"

"It was because of Ezra. Years earlier, he had done something to pay Ezra back. I thought that he had stolen something or had written something into the business contract that had taken advantage of Ezra. Lucas was like that. He could be shrewd with fine details. He wasn't above burying a clause in the middle of a contract that would ensure he got everything he wanted. But I don't know the details. All I know is that well after Ezra's death, we had to run that night, and something had come back to bite him. He thought he could outrun it."

The air grew lighter as the sun rose. Shane still wasn't sure if this was what they were looking for. Mrs. Talbot's lack of details would provide him little ammunition for fighting against Mr. Shadow.

"Do you know the name Mr. Shadow?" Shane asked.

"No," Melissa replied. "Should I?"

"Hard to say," Shane said. "So, what happened the night you fled?"

"Lucas said we needed distance between us and the house. Not much. We booked a room at the Tiverton Inn. He promised we could check in on the children the next day and everything would be fine."

"But you never made it that far," Ventura said.

"I remember being too anxious to eat, but also so exhausted from everything that I just wanted to sleep. Lucas told me to take a nap, and everything would be fine in the morning. I never woke up."

"Someone found you," Ventura said.

"*Something* did," Melissa corrected. "But I never saw it or heard it. And when I came back as this thing, I saw the room. I saw my body there in the bed. And I saw Lucas."

"He was dead as well?"

"They had brutalized him. Much worse than what had happened to me. It was inhuman. Not even animals are slaughtered that way. He was a fool. He was a liar and a cheat, and I will never forgive him for what he did to our family. But nothing he did in life deserved such cruelty."

"I'm very sorry, ma'am," James said. "It's a terrible thing to be punished for the crimes of another."

"I stayed with him. Even when I knew what sort of man he was. I could have resisted that night or left on my own. I made my bed. But the children didn't do anything. They were children! How could someone have done that to my little boy? What did they gain from hurting him like that?"

"I wish I had an answer for you," James told her.

"The person we're looking for is the one who killed your son," Shane said. "A ghost, I think. Probably the same one who came for you that night. Or at least sent someone to do it. He's the one who took Brandy Jean as well."

"He killed her?" Mrs. Talbot asked.

He had not. The ghosts of Shane's house had done that. But in a way, Mr. Shadow was just as responsible if not more so. He had put Beatrix on that path. He had warped her from childhood to be a hunter. To track and kill.

"She's dead, yes," Shane said.

Mrs. Talbot covered her mouth with her hand and looked away, facing north with her back to the three living men. Shane gave her a moment, though she must have known that her daughter's story hadn't ended well.

He wasn't sure how much he trusted Mrs. Talbot's tale. The fact that she readily admitted she could have done more than she had made Shane suspicious. Leaving her children behind on the word of her unreliable husband didn't seem like something a rational person would do. Of course, maybe she wasn't rational. None of it mattered anymore. The decision was made, and consequences were rendered.

"Sorry to have disturbed you, ma'am," James said, bringing the conversation to a close. Shane agreed that it was time to move on. They would not get anything else useful from her.

The ghost said nothing as they walked away. They put some distance between themselves and her before anyone spoke again.

"If they were importing haunted items, my father would have known about it," James said at the cemetery's border.

"Rival business?" Ventura asked.

"In a sense. My father would not have cared about competition. But if they were reckless, importing dangerous spirits and handling them incorrectly, that would have made him angry. Certainly enough to cut off business with both men."

"Maybe they wanted things your old man wouldn't provide, so they set up shop to backdoor his operation. Deacon's papers made it seem like your old man cheated him, right?" Shane said.

"My father did not cheat clients," James said, "but you're right. He would not provide haunted items irresponsibly. Deacon sounded like he grew more unhinged over time. If my father recognized that, he might have cut him off."

"Which set Deacon off and prompted him to go into business with Talbot until that fell apart," Ventura said.

"Deacon scams Talbot somehow, and Talbot gets revenge. Deacon dies brutally at some point, and then years later, the same thing happens to Talbot," Shane finished.

"How?" James asked.

"Mr. Shadow," Ventura said.

"Mr. Shadow kills Deacon in Syracuse. Somehow, years after the fact, he winds up in Rhode Island and kills Talbot. But if Shadow works for himself, how did he get involved? What did Deacon and Talbot do to him that made him want them both dead?" Shane said.

"And what makes him want me dead now?" James added.

Shane looked to the east. The rising sun was still hidden behind the trees. The view was much better from the beach.

"Let's go to the beach house," he said. "See who's still haunting the rubble."

CHAPTER 13
OF SHADOWS

Roy walked down the dark stretch of hallway to the door at the end. The man in the second-to-last cell had been screaming for nearly an hour. Roy had never experienced anything like it, and a part of him wanted to request that they not commit to the changeover just yet.

A human's capacity to endure pain had limitations. Roy had seen both ends of the spectrum many times. Some would break down within seconds, having endured only the most trivial amount of pain. Others could withstand abuse that had killed lesser men without a sound. The range of tolerance fascinated him.

He strived to learn what allowed someone to flirt so closely with death. What made somebody cling to life when a dozen others who had endured the same had died? He had to be able to discover some quantifiable thing. At least he hoped so.

Their latest subject was probably ready for the changeover. He was probably ready to become a Hound. No, not probably, he was. But he had fought more than any other subject. Most lost consciousness at some point. Not this man. He faced it all and screamed himself hoarse, but he lived. He stayed awake. He was remarkable.

Roy would not ask to keep the man alive. He knew Mr. Shadow was not interested in scientific curiosities. Mr. Shadow had no empathy, curiosity, or patience. He wanted things done, and Roy was there to do them. As a professional, Roy did not question the needs of his employer. He fulfilled his task to the best of his abilities. That was part of the reason he was the best at what he did. Still, he was not above lamenting the loss of an anomaly.

The door at the end of the hall opened easily, and Roy stepped inside into the pitch-black room. Although the basement was always cold, this room was like a freezer. Roy had never grown accustomed to the cold of that particular room; it had a biting quality that was hard to shake. Even when he distanced his mind from the sensation, the prickling iciness always drew him back.

"It's time for the changeover," he said into the darkness.

The darkness moved. Roy felt his pulse quicken. Part of his job involved informing Mr. Shadow as they reached new stages. He would give an update and then return to his work. On rare occasions, Mr. Shadow offered instructions. He had not moved, though, until now.

Roy did not scare easily but that did not mean he had no fear. He was of the mind that a person without fear was a person destined for a premature death. There were many things in the world to be afraid of. Roy had seen several of them firsthand.

He could control his fear and focus on other tasks even while being aware of it. That was a skill that took practice. To avoid the fight-or-flight instinct and focus on something else was not a skill that came naturally.

Mr. Shadow frightened Roy. He could not explain how the ghost induced such fear. Still, he did his job the best he could while ignoring it.

The unnatural darkness of the room pulled itself together. It drew into a central form, a denser mass of darkness. It was not a ghost in the traditional sense, not the figure of a wretched old man, a gunshot victim, or any of the hundreds of other ghosts Roy had seen many times before. It was amorphous emptiness.

"Show me," came the voice from nothingness. Roy nodded and left the room.

The darkness trailed after him, sucking in the faint light from the hallway as he led it toward the room where the screaming man waited. Roy unlocked the door and stepped inside. Mr. Shadow followed behind.

His name had been Harlan, but he was not the same person he had been when Roy took him from outside the gym. He couldn't rightly be called Harlan anymore. Roy strongly believed that there came a point when the person no longer existed, and only the thing Roy had created was left. Harlan was gone now; what was left was something broken and defiled.

"I believe all your specifications were followed," Roy said.

Roy did not work on the physical part of creating the Hounds. The design was Mr. Shadow's. The desire and intention were all him. Roy just facilitated the changeover. Roy made ghosts; that was his job.

The man who was once Harlan had been broken down very carefully. He was on antibiotics, hormones, medications, and IV fluids to keep him alive and stave off the infections from his endless wounds and broken bones. Some were standard treatments available at any hospital. Others were devised by Roy and known only to him. They facilitated the transition well.

Electronic monitors kept track of Harlan's heart rate and brainwave activity so Roy could see that he was still alive and that his vitals were declining. He would not live much longer. Roy had witnessed death enough to know that once Mr. Shadow was done, the man would expire. He probably had fewer than five minutes to live.

The design of this one was new, as all Mr. Shadow's designs were. He never wanted the same result. The thing that had once been called Harlan's fingers had been sewn together, the flesh cut and then stitched so five fingers became three. Muscles across the man's body were repositioned. Flesh was peeled back and new muscle was sewn on, harvested from the bodies of other victims.

The drugs used to prevent tissue rejection only needed to last as long as the man did. When he died, it wouldn't matter if his body didn't take to what had been done to it. It was a game of moments. As long as he lived and held his form until the changeover, that was all that mattered. That was where Roy's expertise was involved.

There was still one Hound in the room with the dying man. Its body was merged with the dying man's, embedded in him. The ghost's presence was necessary for the changeover to work the way Roy needed it to. The way Mr. Shadow required it to.

The man who had once been called Harlan was lying on his side on the floor. They hadn't needed to restrain him for some time. His body lacked the ability to move any longer. It was all he could do to keep breathing and screaming. He was covered in sweat and blood. The air in the room smelled foul from all he had endured. There was very little left to do.

"Is he ready?" Mr. Shadow asked.

"Yes," Roy said.

The black morass drifted toward the nearly dead man on the floor. The Hound immersed in the barely living man's body watched its creator reverently.

From within the darkness, an appendage like a tentacle of shadows snaked out and pulled tightly. The form changed from a loose, soft, shadowy bundle to the defined shape of a human arm and hand.

The hand's index finger extended, and the tip curved like a surgical scalpel, glossy and black. The Hound held the man who had once been called Harlan steady as Mr. Shadow's razor-sharp fingertip traced the outline of his lips, cutting them away to expose teeth and gums beneath.

Despite all the suffering he had endured, the man screamed anew as pain was ignited within his body once more. He fought, weak as he was, but he had no strength left. He could do nothing to save his life anymore.

Mr. Shadow peeled the lips from the man's face and tossed them aside like garbage. He moved to the eyes next, carving through the flesh with simple precision. The shadowy implement slid under skin and muscle and meticulously peeled them from the bone. What remained was clean, smooth, and white.

The man who had once been called Harlan began convulsing.

"He's going to die," Roy said to the Hound. "Do as you have been instructed."

As the last tremors of a dying seizure racked the man's body, the Hound plunged its arms and legs into the flesh. The ghost twisted its body back and forth as though struggling. Monitors attached to the dying man beeped, and then the flat line appeared along with the warning tone. His heart had stopped.

Roy and Mr. Shadow watched in silence. The Hound made no noise either, even as it struggled and pulled at the dead man's body. The process, once he was dead, was short. Roy had timed it with others, and it had never taken longer than thirty seconds. This one was much faster, fourteen seconds by his watch.

The Hound pulled up, dragging itself from the man's body but not alone. The Hound surfaced and dragged with it the ghostly form of the dead man that lay on the ground at their feet.

In some ways, it was like witnessing a birth, something dragged from a body to see the world for the first time. The new Hound was wrenched free of the dead flesh that once housed it and tossed onto the ground. The ghost was still for a moment and then slowly got to its feet, looking at Roy and Mr. Shadow with empty eyes.

The Hound screamed. With a body that no longer needed to draw in air, nothing stopped the sound of horror that escaped from the creature's ruined mouth.

Roy smiled. His theories had proven correct. The presence of the old Hound, the merging of the ghost with the dying body, ensured that a new spirit would be pulled from it. They would waste no more subjects on the gamble of whether they would return as Hounds. He felt comfortable making the guarantee to Mr. Shadow. Every subject would meet the changeover successfully. He could create an army in weeks.

"So, you see," Roy said, his voice hard to hear over the Hound's endless scream. "We will now have a hundred percent success rate."

"Continue," Mr. Shadow ordered.

Roy nodded and left the room. His work with the Hound was done, but Mr. Shadow still had to tame the beast. It was newly born, so it was wild and would want to escape or try to be the person it once was. Mr. Shadow would quickly crush that urge. He would make it a loyal Hound like the others, another soldier that obeyed orders without question.

Roy closed the door behind him and proceeded down the hall to the next room. Once he had overseen several more changeovers, he would feel comfortable handing over the bulk of the duties to some of the Harvesters. The first round needed the personal touch. Soon enough, though, they would scale up. They needed to find more subjects.

CHAPTER 14

FROM ASHES

Shane took the lead and drove across Tiverton to the secluded road that led to the house on the beach. Some things had changed since his last visit, if only slightly. The house that had once stood near the shore had been burned down to little more than a black spot in the sand. Police had set caution tape around it to keep anyone from exploring the ruins and potentially hurting themselves.

"I should return home soon," James said as Shane pulled the car to a stop near the house. "I have some of my father's old files there, things I thought were unrelated to the business. If there was a personal grudge, there might be mention of Talbot or Deacon in them. Maybe something to help us find Mr. Shadow."

"You sure you want to go back to your house now?" Shane asked as they left the vehicle and joined Ventura.

"We need some answers instead of more questions," James said.

"But there's a good chance Shadow has your house staked out. He's got to know his hit squad from last night failed. This guy has the patience to hunt his target for a long time."

"James probably has our best shot at finding some leads," Ventura countered. "This is before all our times. His father is the best link we have."

"Maybe," Shane said, "but Shadow once lived in this house. Ghosts here knew him. If anyone's left, that's a firsthand, almost living account. Worth a look, right?"

"Yes, of course," James agreed.

"So long as they're not pissed at you for burning it down," Ventura offered as they left the road and walked across the sand.

A handful of burned, black timbers stood upright at the back corners of the house, but most of it was gone. The upper floors had collapsed, and the foundation was surrounded by ash and charred rubble.

The basement was no longer visible from the outside as it had been filled in with the burned remnants of the house. That meant there was still room hidden beneath things, places where haunted items could have fallen. Places where ghosts could still lurk.

As the three crossed the ash-speckled sand toward the house, Shane saw a familiar figure standing in the surf. The ghost he had seen on his first visit was still there, still in the water nearby.

"You know him?" Ventura asked as Shane detoured toward the ghost standing ankle-deep in wet sand.

"We met. He's not the most helpful spirit, but he wasn't outright hostile. He might know something."

Shane lifted a hand and waved at the ghost as he approached, stopping just out of reach of the waves rolling into shore and several feet from the ghost.

"You came back," the ghost observed. "Nothing left to burn down."

"Still need information," Shane said. "About the people who used to live here. The Talbots."

"I don't know any Talbots," the ghost replied.

Water dripped from the ghost's long coat. His flesh was pale and swollen, hanging in saturated blobs from his frame and looking like they might tear off under their own weight at any moment. Wounds across his face and hands were glistening and red but no blood flowed, having long since been washed away with the tide.

"The ones who used to live in the house. The boy, Ben, was their son. Brandy Jean was their daughter," Shane explained.

"I don't know any Talbots," the ghost repeated.

Shane sighed, glancing back at the house.

"You never saw—"

"I don't know anything," the ghost said, interrupting him. "I saw what you did here. I don't want anything to do with you. You want to know something? Go ask the two you left behind."

He pointed a pasty, bloated finger at the burned-out house.

"Two, huh?" Shane said. "Sure."

He'd not gotten an accurate count of ghosts in the house when he was there. It had reminded him of the house on Berkley Street in a lot of ways, though. Several ghosts were present, and the effect they had on the house was harrowing. At the time, Shane wasn't positive he would escape the house alive.

They left the drowned ghost behind and returned to the ruins of Beatrix's old home. Part of the wraparound deck was still present at the rear of the house, charred along the edges. The steps that led from the sandy beach to what was once a sliding glass door were still intact. Now, they were behind flimsy, yellow tape and led to nothing.

Shane pulled aside the tape and walked up the three steps to the rickety porch, looking down at the burned remains of the building. Ventura and James joined him, standing on the porch and taking in the destruction.

"Is there something I'm meant to see?" Ventura asked.

"Anything that looks back at you," Shane suggested.

It would be too dangerous to cross the burn threshold and navigate the building. Much of what he could see were stacks of busted, half-burned timbers. He couldn't tell whether there was an intact floor underneath it. Even if there was, it had probably weakened enough that they would fall through if they entered. Shane had been attacked by a ghost in the basement here more than once already, and he didn't want to go through it again.

"There," James said, pointing to the northern corner of the house.

It was the largest portion of the house still standing. There were fragments of wall on either side of a corner post, the tallest bit maybe four feet from the ground. Huddled in the corner, knees up, with eyes staring back at Shane, was a small ghost that he hadn't seen before when he was in the house.

The spirit looked like that of a teenage girl. She was frail, with thin arms and legs, and dressed in black. Dark hair hung in her face and cascaded about her shoulders. As Shane watched, the strands looked like they moved on their own, gently swaying and writhing about.

"Hello," Shane greeted her.

The porch near where she sat was too badly burned for him to approach. He walked out as far as he dared, stopping before the pale, sun-bleached wood was replaced by the fragmented, burned, black planks.

"What do you want?" she asked.

Her tone was curt and though Shane hadn't recalled seeing her during his first visit, it was possible that she had seen him and knew he was responsible for burning the place down.

"Information," he said. "I need to know about the Talbots."

"They're all mostly dead now," she said. "Except Brandy Jean."

"She's dead," Shane corrected. "I need to know about her parents."

The girl stared at him suspiciously.

"She was just here. When you were," she said.

"Yeah. Then she tried to kill me again. Didn't work out," he explained.

"You killed her?"

"Not personally. Other ghosts did," Shane answered.

The girl chuckled and nodded approvingly.

"Good."

"Not a fan, I take it," Shane said.

"She was mean for no reason. I never liked her."

"What about her parents?"

The ghost shrugged.

"Didn't know the mom. She couldn't see spirits. The father was… he was strange. I didn't like him, either. Better than Deacon, I guess."

"You knew Ezra Deacon?" James asked.

"I used to be stuck in his house. Kept me there until Mr. Talbot came one day. He took me and a bunch more back here, left us in this place. Almost every ghost in this house came from Deacon," she said.

"What happened to Deacon?" James asked. "Why did he allow Talbot to take you?"

"Never allowed anything. He was dead by then," the ghost explained.

"Did Talbot kill him?" Shane asked.

She shook her head. "A ghost killed old Ezra Deacon. He pushed his luck with the wrong person, and they got revenge. Plain and simple."

"Mr. Shadow?" Shane asked.

The girl smirked, her eyes locked on Shane's, and she chuckled again.

"*Mister* Shadow," she said sarcastically, emphasizing the first word like a joke only she understood. "Of course not."

"Why do you say that?" Shane asked.

"Because they were in love. Shadow and Deacon were thick as thieves and creepy, even if no one ever said it out loud. Ghost and a living man all lovey-dovey like that. It was uncomfortable and odd."

Shane had not expected to hear that. He looked at James and saw surprise and confusion as well. If Shadow and Deacon were in love, that put a new spin on the dynamic but still explained so little.

"I'm sorry. So, you're saying this Mr. Shadow and Ezra Deacon were romantically involved?" James asked.

"Until Deacon died, yes. He was a bad man who did bad things, but Shadow didn't care. Why would she? She was just as twisted. But Deacon wouldn't stop pressing Moran about ripping him off, and Moran must have gotten sick of it. Sent him a package with a ghost inside that killed him. So long, Ezra Deacon. Talbot was there soon after and saved a lot of us, but it was too late for Deacon."

"A ghost assassin?" James said, his voice thick with disbelief. "That's impossible."

"Tell that to Deacon," the girl said.

James turned to Shane and Ventura, his jaw set and anger brewing behind his eyes.

"My father was an efficient man and sometimes even harsh, but he was no killer. He never would have sent a ghost to assassinate someone, especially over a business dispute. Good Lord, half the reason he did what he did was to prevent irresponsible and monstrous acts like that."

"Your father?" the girl in the corner said. "You're Moran's son?"

"I am, and your story is flawed. If you were trapped in a box in Deacon's collection, how would you know who killed him?"

The ghost stood, her hair writhing faster, more agitated.

"I don't need to answer questions from someone like you. I know enough," she replied, her voice low and angry.

She rushed from the ashes, coming for James with her pale, thin fingers extended like the claws of a bird of prey. James took a step back as Shane put himself between the two, catching the girl by the shoulders and pushing her back before she could attack.

"Just here for information; this doesn't need to get uglier than it is," he told her.

In the burned rubble behind her, Shane saw another ghost was now present. It gave no indication that it intended to join the fray, preferring to stand silently, watch, and listen.

"His father killed Ezra Deacon. We all saw the package he sent. It had his name right on it!" the girl ghost hissed.

"The hallmark of any good assassin, a return address," James said with no small degree of sarcasm.

The ghost came for him again, and Shane caught her arm and tried to hold her steady. She was incredibly thin, but she pulled and fought like a wild animal. Shane held fast, and she clawed at his arms, hissing and cursing as she scratched and kicked at him to get free.

103

Shane cursed as he felt her nails dig into the flesh of his arm. He grabbed her other wrist and held her steady as best as he could, but she focused on her legs and kicked out more, scraping thick toenails down his inner thighs and across his gut.

"I need you to calm down and talk to us. How do you know it was James' father? What happened to Deacon?"

"And why did you refer to Mr. Shadow as 'she'?" Ventura added.

"He sold ghosts. He sold the boxes lined with lead, and that's what he sent to Deacon. I saw it after; the package and the box. Everyone saw. Everyone knew!"

She thrashed again in Shane's grip and this time reversed course, coming toward him instead of pulling away. Her hair wrapped around Shane's face. It tangled like a net to the back of his neck, and he felt her teeth dig into his throat as the nest of hair tied them together.

Shane yelled in pain and released her wrists, focusing instead on her head. He tried to push her away, but her teeth were sunk into his throat. Even pulling back the hair proved fruitless as it twisted about his fingers like a thousand tiny snakes.

Her jaw flexed, and he felt her trying to bring her teeth together. Her mouth was small and weak. The bite had not hit an artery, but she was trying to pull a chunk free. Shane pressed his hands to either side of her head and turned his neck as much as her jaws and hair would allow. He closed his eyes as he brought his hands together.

The ghost's skull crunched and burst. The blast knocked Shane back off the wraparound porch and onto the wet sand of the beach. He landed hard, feeling hot blood run down his shoulder from his neck.

Ventura was quickly at his side, a handkerchief at the ready. He pressed the fabric to Shane's wound but Shane waved him away, taking over for himself as he sat up.

"She bit you," Ventura said.

"I noticed," Shane replied.

"She had to be lying," James said, ignoring Shane's injury.

Shane got to his feet, holding the square of white cloth to the bite on his neck, and nodded.

"It sounds a little flimsy. Ghost sent through the mail is not the most convincing plot."

There were, of course, bigger problems in the ghost's story. Where had the assassin spirit gone after it killed Deacon? It had turned him into a Hound, or at least an early version of one, which meant it was linked to Mr. Shadow. But the ghost insisted that Mr. Shadow and Deacon were in love. And, as Ventura pointed out, she had called Mr. Shadow "she".

Before Shane could voice any questions, the burned house's foundation began to shake.

CHAPTER 15
PAST SINS

James stepped down from the wraparound porch as the remnants of the house continued to rumble. The broken and burned timbers moved, but not the way they were supposed to. They pulled themselves together, growing and shedding the ash from the fire to reveal clean, solid wood.

Support beams and pillars rose. The frame of the house rebuilt itself and then the panels filled in with insulation, drywall, and siding. The first floor gave rise to the second floor, and finally, the attic and roof rebuilt themselves from the ashes.

The reformed house was not the building that Shane had previously visited. That was a rundown, abandoned beach house that suffered from neglect, weather, and time. The thing that built itself in front of Shane and the others was the house as it must have been when it was new. Every bit was clean, pristine, and perfect. There was no flaking paint or weather-worn panels. It was brand new and beautiful.

As the rumbling settled and the rebuild finished, the sliding back door opened. The second ghost they had seen in the ashes stepped onto the porch. The spirit was that of a man Shane did not recognize from his previous visit.

The ghost was dressed in a suit that looked like he might have been buried in it. He was clean-cut and handsome the way movie stars were in black-and-white pictures from back in the day. The only thing that stood out to ruin the image was the bullet wound to the right side of the man's forehead just below his hairline.

"Jeffrey?" James said suddenly, a lack of certainty in his voice.

"James. You've changed," the ghost said.

"It's been forty-five years, give or take," he replied. "I thought… I don't even know. I assume Father found a place for you."

"He did," the ghost replied.

"Mind filling the rest of us in?" Shane interrupted. James raised his eyebrows.

"This is Jeffrey. My father acquired him… God, I don't even remember when. All my earliest memories included him. I didn't even know he was a ghost at the time."

"I was there before you were born," the ghost replied. "I remember the day you came home from the hospital."

"He was always in the store with my father. They talked and played chess all the time. Jeffrey taught me to play," James said.

"You had a ghost nanny. Interesting," Ventura said.

"Not a nanny. More like an uncle, I suppose. Sort of in the background. Until he wasn't. How did you end up here?"

"It was my idea. Your father was troubled by a man named Ezra Deacon, who I gather you are very much aware of now."

"To a degree," James said. "We've been trying to unravel the mystery of that for some time."

"For my part, I suggested your father give me to Deacon. He had already threatened a lawsuit, he was sending harassing letters, and we'd heard from others that he had been violent in the past. I thought it best, since you were still so young, to end things before they escalated. I was a peace offering."

"Peace for what? What agitated Deacon so much?"

"In my time with him, I learned that he was not rational. Anything could set him off. He'd convinced himself that your father was short-changing him on deals, overcharging for inferior haunted items, intentionally sabotaging him, all manner of paranoid fantasies."

"So, he sent you?"

"Something your father valued to show his good intentions. It wasn't who I was or what I could do. It was that losing me would hurt your father. Mr. Deacon took pleasure in something spiteful like that."

"Then why did this girl think my father killed Deacon?"

Jeffrey nodded and looked from James to Shane and Ventura.

"Come," he said. "This house can answer questions better than I can. It is full of memories."

He walked back into the house, leaving the others outside on the sand.

"This can't be a good idea, right?" Ventura asked.

"Your call," Shane said to James. "You trust him?"

"Yes. I mean, I did. I can't speak for the house," James answered.

"The house is a nightmare," Shane said, "but I don't think this is real. Or not fully real. I don't think it has much power left."

"Then let's see what Jeffrey has to say," James said, heading up the stairs to the door.

Shane and Ventura followed across the porch and through the door into the familiar living room. Gone were the oversized cobwebs and stale air. The living room was vibrant with art on the walls and a brilliant shine to the wood floor that made everything warm and welcoming.

Two men entered the room and Ventura tensed, ready to draw his weapon. Shane stopped him. The men were not there, nor were they ghosts. They were illusions, a fantasy like the room. Like the entire house.

"Did you see that monster attached to the Luger?" asked the younger of the two men, a blond fellow with an easy smile and blue eyes. He had to have been Talbot. The resemblance to Beatrix was uncanny.

"Imagine what we could do if we brought these things into the country ourselves. The money, Lucas. The money!" the other man said excitedly.

The two men passed through the living room to the dining room. Shane and his companions followed, watching the illusions sit at the table.

"It's a lot, Ezra. The time. The investment. The danger."

"Danger," the illusion of Ezra Deacon scoffed. He had darker hair, and his features were sharper than Talbot's. He looked severe and critical like the sort of man who got what he wanted more often than not. "The danger is an illusion. Moran's blowing smoke. It's how he makes money."

"That was smoke? That thing?"

"Lead boxes! It's like a muzzle for a dog. These things are all bluster. They can't travel, they can't pass lead, and they can only do what you want them to, you'll see," Deacon explained.

Talbot drank from a bottle of beer and nodded, his enthusiasm growing.

"You know Moran's got to be sitting on better stuff, right? He's got to have some prize stuff hidden away. But the suppliers are what I want. Imagine what they must have in Europe or Asia. Africa! Old ones. We could find a ghost that walked with Pharaohs, Ezra!"

"Walked with?" Deacon laughed. "Hell, we could find the ghost of a Pharoah."

The illusion slipped away like rain running down a wall, and the room was the living room again. Talbot and Deacon were seated, dressed in different clothes. Talbot sported a beard, and time had passed.

"You have to loop me in, that's all I'm saying," Talbot said.

"It's not a big deal, Luke. You either trust me or you don't. This is my business, too."

"I just want to know what's going on."

"I don't ask to see records of who you talk to or where you go," Deacon said, his ire growing. Talbot looked confused.

"I'm not spying on you; they're business deals. I want to know where our money is going."

"Funny how it's always *our* money when I spend it, but it's *your* money when you spend it."

"I was paying off customs," Talbot said sharply. "For us. This stuff isn't regulated. You can't pull gold out of the Congo without someone asking questions. And no one cares if there's the ghost of some old king attached to it, they'll think you're crazy for talking about it."

"I'm not crazy!" Deacon shot back.

He slammed his drink on the table, and the glass shattered. The illusory world shattered with it. The living room became the dining room once more. Both men were present, again dressed in different clothing. Deacon looked tired, with bags under his eyes. Talbot had gained weight.

"The Turk is mine," Deacon said, his voice measured and cold.

"The hell it is. I sourced it. I flew to goddamn Morocco for it. What have you been doing? Building a lead vault like a doomsday maniac? I'm doing the work, Ezra. I'm doing everything."

"I'm giving you one last chance, Lucas Talbot. One way or another, I'm leaving with that haunted mask."

"Go home, Ezra. I'll call you the next time I need a check signed."

Deacon rushed Talbot without warning. Talbot was caught by surprise. The older man rained blows on his face. His fighting style was messy and unrefined. He threw his hands haphazardly, striking Talbot in the nose, cheeks, and even the forehead. Had Talbot any idea how to defend himself, he could have easily overpowered Deacon, but he did not.

Talbot held up a hand to defend himself, blindly reaching with the other until he grabbed the edge of a small, wooden cutting board on the counter. He swung it hard and slammed Deacon in the side of the head, knocking the man to the ground.

"Get the hell out of my house before I kill you," Talbot warned.

Deacon stared at his one-time partner with malice. He scrambled to his feet and stalked out of the room without another word. Talbot cursed and threw the cutting board, which hit the wall and clattered to the floor.

The house faded away, and a new room appeared, one Shane had not seen before. As the details filled in, it became familiar, but not from Rhode Island. It was the house in Syracuse that had belonged to Ezra Deacon.

Deacon was in his vault, sitting on a stool at a workbench. Several envelopes and packages were next to him, and he plucked one from the pile. It was a brown paper envelope addressed to Deacon. The return address, penned in a refined hand, was Moran and Moran.

"That's not my father's handwriting," James said. "The man wrote like he was making recruitment posters. Big, block letters."

Deacon stared at the envelope for a long moment. He was not alone in the house. Ghosts were with him, outside the vault, in the small storage room, and in the hallway beyond. None of them paid Deacon any mind, and he ignored them, too. He pulled open the edge of the package to see what was inside.

A small, sealed box tumbled from the envelope into Deacon's extended hand. Shane recognized the box immediately. It was about the size of a ring box, and a small clasp on three of the four sides held it shut. He had the same box in his pocket.

In the illusion, Deacon opened the box. A ring was inside, pitted and old and very unremarkable to look at. The moment it was free, a ghost manifested in the room alongside Deacon.

From behind, Shane could see the ghost was that of a man. He was not fat but not exactly muscular. He wore a dirty white tank top, exposing his shoulders and part of his back from the rear. His body was covered in sores like he had suffered a severe rash. His flesh was patchy and red, and cracked and oozing in some places.

Beneath the sores, Shane saw old tattoos along the spirit's arms. He guessed they were very plain military tattoos. It looked like the ghost had once been a sailor. He could only see what the illusion showed him, however, as though it had been formed from the memory of someone who had only glimpsed the ghost and then looked away.

The ghost's jeans were faded and dirty, and he wore heavy-looking work boots. He looked like he had died on a construction site, or some other manual labor job. The boots were steel-toed, and the oil stains on the spirit's pants spoke of some dirty and laborious work.

Deacon couldn't utter a word as the ghost attacked him and knocked him to the ground. He broke Deacon's spine with one blow, slamming his foot on the small of the living man's back and shattering it.

Ventura winced as he watched the ghost kick every inch of Deacon from head to toe, breaking bones, and sending blood splattering across the room. One of the ghosts in the hall saw what was happening and called for help, but the spirit savaging Deacon swatted backward with one hand and pushed the door to the vault closed from the inside, shutting them out.

The illusion shifted again, outside of the vault this time, where Talbot appeared. Ghosts moved out of his way and asked him for help, rushing to tell him what had happened and speaking over one another.

Talbot pulled open the vault door and gasped. The ghosts in the hall fell silent save for the ghost of a woman that Shane had not seen before.

She got to her knees on the vault floor, hovering over Ezra Deacon's body. Though he looked dead, he gasped quietly, and it was clear he had survived the beating. The ghost must have intentionally left him alive to extend the suffering. The spirit who had done the work was nowhere to be seen.

"Jesus, Ezra, what happened?" Talbot asked.

The other man was in no position to answer. Multiple bones were broken, and his face was a patchwork of bruises and cuts. That he was alive at all, laying in a pool of his blood, was a miracle.

"Help him," the female ghost begged.

She was older than Deacon, and her voice was panicked. Half her head was covered in thick, honey-colored hair that reached her shoulders. She had been scalped on the other side, exposing her skull. It was bloody, and Shane could only guess how half her head had been torn away.

The woman's face was mostly undamaged. Her eye, under the wounded portion of her head, was severely bloodshot, but nothing else seemed out of place. She wept openly, trying to do something for Ezra with no idea what to do or how to do it.

"I can't," Talbot said, stunned. "I don't know what to do. I…"

He shook his head, taking a step back. While the woman's ghost begged Ezra to live, Talbot turned to the desk and the small ring box. He closed the lid, sealed the clasps, and set it on a shelf before turning to look at the others.

"We have to get out of here," he said.

"What?" the woman's ghost cried. "He's still alive! You have to help him!"

"Look at him, for God's sake. He's dying. And after he dies, they'll come here and take all of this—all of you—somewhere. We have to go back to my house."

"He could come back," the ghost insisted.

Talbot seemed stumped for a moment but then nodded awkwardly.

"Yes, he could. Maybe. I don't know."

"How does it happen?" she demanded.

"What?"

"How? How can we make sure he comes back? He needs to come back!"

"Doctor—" Talbot began.

The ghost rose to her feet and took Talbot by the throat. Her nails were like knives, pointed and sharp just below his jaw.

"Tell me!" she screamed.

"It's not… I mean, there's no guarantee," Talbot explained. "Trauma? Violence? What happened to him might cause him to cross over. I don't know."

"Trauma," the ghost said, turning back to Deacon. "Yes. Trauma."

Chapter 16
In the Flesh

Talbot began collecting boxes from inside Deacon's vault, opening some to take smaller haunted items and releasing the spirits within. Shane didn't recognize anything. Whatever Talbot had taken, it had not been returned, and Shane had not discovered it anywhere else. Talbot carried as much as he could and left the ghost of the woman weeping over Deacon's dying body.

"This must have been the last thing he opened," Talbot said, indicating the envelope. The other ghosts looked at it. Shane recognized some from the house, including the girl he'd just been forced to destroy.

"Moran," one of the ghosts said.

The weeping woman looked over her shoulder as the others spoke about what happened.

"It's sealed away now," Talbot said, calming everyone, "but we have to go."

He left, taking everything he could carry from the room.

The illusion shimmered just barely. Talbot was back, and the ghost of the woman was kneeling over Deacon's body. Shane and the others watched as she used the edge of her fingernail to slice into the man's already brutalized flesh. He didn't make a sound as she cut deep, drawing blood.

"What the hell are you doing?" Talbot asked as he approached.

The ghost dug and cut, removing slices of flesh from his face and peeling away muscle and tissue down to the bone.

"Saving him," she whispered. "You said this will save him."

"What?" Talbot muttered, watching in horror as the ghost flayed Deacon's still-living face.

"Trauma can bring him back. He needs the pain to come back to me," she whispered.

"Jesus Christ, not like that!" Talbot shouted. "You can't... it doesn't work like that. You can't torture a ghost into existence."

He grabbed more haunted items off the shelves in the vault and backed away as Deacon's body convulsed.

"Yes!" the woman cried, lifting his body from the ground like a puppet, holding him as he writhed in her ghostly grip. "Come back to me, my love. Come back."

Blood poured down Deacon's half-missing face. A gurgle escaped his lips, and his body went limp. The ghost couldn't hold him up any longer, and he flopped to the floor, outside the vault at Talbot's feet.

"Jesus," the living man muttered. He took one last box from the vault, snapping the lid closed, and causing the woman who had cut off Deacon's face to vanish.

Barely a moment passed when something began to manifest inside the vault. Shane had not seen the moment of rebirth for many spirits, and never one so badly traumatized as Deacon had been. But he had seen the result of this one's return.

The flayed face coalesced from nothing along with the broken and bruised body. Deacon's ghost howled a piercing and inhuman sound. Talbot shook his head.

"My God," he said. "Not like this. What is this?"

He pushed the vault door closed as Deacon's ghost pulled itself together in monstrous, nightmare form. The door slammed shut, cutting off the horrible sounds, but Talbot didn't know the code to seal it. Instead, he covered it with the hidden closet panel, disguising it from view.

"We've got to clean this up and go now," Talbot said to the other ghosts before the illusion faded once more.

The illusion became the beach house next. Talbot was there with his boxes and haunted items, placing them around the ghosts. The ghosts he'd taken from Deacon seemed to know him. They didn't fight or attack. They settled in, becoming part of the house.

Shane recognized the burned ghost that had attacked him in the basement. The pale one from under the bed. The one called Spider. The girl from the corner, Jeffrey, and a handful of others. All part of Talbot's house from that point on.

"What happened to the ghost of the woman?" Shane asked, not seeing her among the others.

Jeffrey walked out of the illusion, causing it to fade, and then it returned as the room in the basement where Shane had first met Beatrix's brother Ben. It was a cold, empty space, with no drawings on the walls yet. A small, lead-lined container was on a table.

"He kept her here," Jeffrey explained. "For many years after. When Deacon died, a darkness grew in her and would not go away. Nothing could stop it. Mr. Talbot feared her, so he kept her locked away."

"Who was she?" James asked.

Jeffrey shrugged.

"I don't know. A doctor of some kind. A surgeon, I think. But she was cruel and cold. Maybe they admired that in one another, her and Ezra Deacon. They could both be so callous. Vengeful. I think they loved one another in their own way. Some dark form of love, anyway. But they brought out the worst in each other, too, and they thrived on it. She fed his madness and paranoia. His downward spiral had always been her."

"Until he died," Shane said.

"He died, and she brought him back. Just not as he was," Jeffrey said.

"She became Mr. Shadow," Shane said. "Talbot's kids freed her. They were like their dad. They could see ghosts. Sense them. But they were more than he was. And Shadow had become something else, too."

"Talbot had to have been the one who sent the package to Deacon,"

Ventura said. "He framed your father because it was easy. It would have fed into the paranoia that Deacon already felt. And it allowed Talbot to swoop in as the hero. None of the ghosts even protested him coming to take them away."

"Mr. Shadow was an unexpected side effect of a business relationship gone bad," James said. "This was always about greed. For money, more haunted items, and control of the business."

"At first," Shane agreed. "When he had children, Mr. Talbot sealed away everyone he deemed dangerous. They were imprisoned in the basement. But the house had absorbed much by then, and he didn't seal everyone away. The house had a will of its own. It wanted the ghosts to be found. And since the children were so sensitive to them, it allowed them to find the hidden prisons."

"Beatrix and Ben released everyone, including Mr. Shadow. She had become something else after all that time," Jeffrey said. "A sweeping, malevolent darkness. She killed the boy soon after. She kept the girl. Molded her into something useful."

"This was a revenge plot from the beginning. From thirty-odd years ago," Ventura said. "But James' father was long since dead, so why pick the son?"

"Because that's what dark things do," Shane answered.

"She wanted blood," Jeffrey agreed. "Talbot tried to escape, to travel beyond her grasp. But he underestimated her influence. She didn't need to kill him, she just needed to find a ghost that was closer to him who could do it for her. And it worked. She influences those who listen. She did it to Deacon, and Talbot's daughter. She'll kill or use anyone to get what she wants."

"And what does she want?" James asked.

"For now, it looks like you," Shane said. "Everything with Beatrix and hunting ghosts that had come from you, or people linked to you, was meant to draw you out. I think she chose now because she finally figured out how to make this thing with the Hounds work. Deacon was a fluke, but it sparked the idea."

"Why does she want to make Hounds?" Ventura asked.

"She sends them to hunt and kill. That's what she wants. To hurt as many people as she can. It won't stop with James."

"Do you know where Shadow is now?" James asked the ghost.

Jeffrey shook his head.

"Brandy Jean—Beatrix—took her from here long ago. They didn't have much use for the rest of us, so they just left us here with the boy's ghost. They knew he could destroy us if we got out of line. Now that all of it's gone, I don't think anyone's coming back."

"We need to find out where Beatrix would have taken the ghost. Maybe another one of Deacon's properties," Shane suggested. "Someplace private and secluded. You can't skin faces to make Hounds in a townhouse complex."

"I should head back to the office," Ventura said. "I can see what else might fit the bill that was under Ezra Deacon's name, or his granddaughter's name."

"There might be something in my father's personal files as well," James added. "If things were as bad as they seemed with Deacon, he probably would have kept some records for legal reasons."

Shane was eager enough to leave Rhode Island. They were making progress, and he hoped to keep the momentum going. Mr. Shadow no longer had allies, no one doing the leg work the way Beatrix had. If there were still Harvesters around, they were low-ranking. Shane doubted they would be reliable or good for much. Not if they were like the ones he'd found at James' shop. Mr. Shadow would need a new apprentice if she wanted to keep her work going.

As long as Mr. Shadow remained obsessed with finding Moran, there would be an opportunity to track her down. As long as everyone stayed alive.

"I can take you back with us," James said to Jeffery.

The ghost laughed, and the illusion of the house vanished. They were on the beach again, looking at the burned foundation.

"My haunted item is buried under ten feet of burned wood and water. I don't think I'll be leaving anytime soon."

James nodded, sensing from Shane and Ventura the urgency to leave. He told the ghost that he would be back, and the three of them left.

"I'm heading to the field office in Boston," Ventura said before heading to his vehicle. "I'll call when I have something. Keep in touch, and do not break into any more houses."

"I'll see what I can do," Shane said, shaking the man's hand.

"I'm going home," James told him, shaking hands as well. "We'll be in touch."

Ventura left quickly while Shane and James were a short distance behind. They drove north, heading to James' house instead of the shop. Shane had spent little time at James' home, though he had been there once or twice. James was typically private about his personal life, but everything with Mr. Shadow and the Harvesters had brought many things to the forefront.

"I don't think Mr. Shadow will believe us if we try to explain that my father had nothing to do with Deacon's murder," James said while they drove.

"I imagine not," Shane agreed.

"Which means either she kills me, or we destroy her."

"That's the long and short of it," Shane said. That was probably the only outcome from the moment he heard the name Mr. Shadow. Ghosts like that were not the sort to listen to reason. She had transformed into a nightmare bent on curating and developing a breed of monstrous spirits. All because of a need for revenge from decades ago. Destroying her was the only option.

"We're going to have to make this quick," Shane said, changing the subject. "She probably knows where you live. If there aren't Harvesters waiting for us, they'll be there soon if they know we're back in town."

"I'll try to be fast," James assured him, "but we're still flying blind here."

"Yeah, but speed works to our advantage. If nothing else, we know that Shadow is a very slow plotter. She might not be able to keep up if we keep making progress."

"Possibly," James said. "Though I do wonder what's kept her busy all these years."

CHAPTER 17

LOOKING BACK

"Why do you think Mr. Shadow kept Beatrix alive?" James asked.

They had been in James' house for the better part of the day. Shane stood in the hallway while James dug through old file boxes in a closet. Everything was neatly labeled as belonging to his father, including date ranges for the files within. If nothing else, his organization would make finding things easier if there was anything to find.

"Because of her brother," Shane said. "The boy came back dangerous. Dangerous like when he was alive. I think it was the first time Shadow realized that being a ghost didn't mean being invulnerable. Ben died, but Beatrix was raised and trained to be a ghost hunter, a weapon. Together, with the Hounds, they would have been able to take on almost anything."

"But who?" James asked, opening a box of files, and pulling out folders. "Who did she think they were going to war with?"

"Anyone. Everyone," Shane said. "Deacon was paranoid, right? And your friend Jeffrey said she rubbed off on him. She might have seen enemies around every corner after Deacon was killed."

"Perhaps," James said, scanning the papers. "To think so many people have had to die over this. Innocent people caught up in feuds from before they were born."

"I'm not sure there's as much of a plan here as we think, either. Beatrix was very haphazard in how she conducted business. Distracted, even. I think Mr. Shadow might be the same way. Vengeance moves to the back burner in favor of focusing on the girl who can fight ghosts. And she gets back-burnered in favor of the Hounds," Shane said.

He'd already seen that Beatrix's second-in-command, Lanthimos, had lost faith in the process and gone rogue, bringing a group of Hounds to attack Shane and ultimately help destroy Ben. There was no great organizational structure. It seemed like impulse.

That made sense in a way. Jeffrey had said Shadow had become something darker after Deacon's death, and after being hidden away. Shane had seen things happen like that. Lazarus, from the Iron Tournament, had succumbed to the darkness of a thousand victims over the ages.

Ghosts could fall into despair and manifest their hate and anger. It became them and guided them. Rational thought sometimes got lost along the way.

"The Hounds," James repeated. "Wherever those are being made is where we'll find Mr. Shadow. It must be something secluded. How many properties could Deacon have owned?"

"No guarantee it was one of his properties. It could have been something Talbot owned. Or something else. Beatrix could have bought a place for Shadow. We saw how much cash Deacon had in his vault, so Shadow knows how to get money," Shane pointed out.

James was right that it needed to be secluded. The number of people Shadow must be killing to make new Hounds meant they would need a lot of privacy. But that didn't narrow the field.

The only thing Shane knew for certain was that Mr. Shadow was still not working alone. Even without Beatrix, others were taking up the slack. People—like the three who had come after James with their Hound the day before—needed to go out and find victims.

Inside the closet, James stuffed the folder back into its file box and pushed it aside. He grabbed a second box and rifled through it before sighing loudly and shaking his head.

"There's nothing here," he said, frustrated. "We've wasted an entire day."

Outside, the sun had already begun to set. James had looked through more boxes and cabinets and trunks than Shane thought one man could have. They had scoured the basement and the attic before heading to the closet in which he'd stored what he thought were just tax records and old bills.

"Do you think you'll find anything if we keep looking?"

"It's all useless," he replied, pushing the first box. "He did business with Talbot and Deacon; we know that. Deacon sued him and then dropped the case; we know that. There's nothing else. These men meant nothing to my father, and he had nothing to do with their business or squabbles."

"Then it's like we thought," Shane said. "The ghost was probably sent by Talbot. He used your father as a fall guy to cover his ass."

"And how many people are dead now because of it?" James said.

There was anger in his voice, subtle though it might have been. James Moran was typically the picture of calm. He was rational and level, and he allowed logic and reason to guide him whenever possible. But this cut too close to home.

"At least—" Shane began, stopping as the lights in the house flickered.

James was on his feet in an instant. The power fluctuated one last time and then died. The house went black.

Shane stood still, looking down the hall towards James' living room. Light curtains covered the window, but a shape moved outside in the failing light.

"On your six, Ryan."

The voice preceded a faint creak in the floorboards. Shane turned to see Xander Ventura behind him with a gun drawn.

"This you?" Shane asked, gesturing to the lights.

"No. Just showed up to see if you guys had found anything and saw the van parked out front. Pair of well-armed gentlemen are making their way to the front door with a Hound in tow. Figured I'd come in through the back and offer a hand."

"Why didn't you just shoot them out front?" Shane asked.

Ventura stared at him in silence for a beat. Before he could reply, something hit the front door, and the sound of splintered wood preceded the appearance of a man with a gun. He took aim at Shane, but Ventura fired before he could get off a round.

The Harvester took the round in the chest and collapsed. Ventura rushed to check the body. At the same time, Shane heard a click behind him, and ducked then kicked back just before the second Harvester fired.

His boot caught the Harvester in the gut, causing the man to double over. Shane was on him quickly, tackling him and hammering the hand holding his weapon against the floor again and again until he dropped it.

The two men fought, with the Harvester throwing wild punches as Shane slammed an elbow twice into the side of his attacker's face, breaking his jaw. Ventura arrived a moment later when Shane drove his knee into the Harvester's groin. The man cried out in pain, and Ventura lifted him from the ground, then threw him face-down next to Shane, slapping cuffs on his wrists.

"Down," Shane shouted as the agent clicked the second bracelet into place. He took Ventura by the shirt collar and yanked him down as the Hound bounded down the hall toward him.

Shane pushed himself up using Ventura's back to steady himself and met the Hound before it could attack the agent. He slammed his body against the Hound's, driving his shoulder into the ghost's chest.

They fell back together to the floor. The Hound scrambled and slashed at Shane with broken fingernails, making wild, sweeping strikes. It scratched Ventura's leg as he backed away and then dug deep into the back of the restrained Harvester, hooking the man's throat and pulling out a ragged chunk of flesh.

The Harvester's scream died as the Hound severed the artery and blood gushed across James' floor. Shane was on top of the spirit before it could strike out at him again, forcing its head down, and trying to crush it.

"Shane," James shouted.

He lifted his head as a second Hound appeared in the doorway near the man Ventura had shot. Another followed behind it, and Shane cursed.

"Back door. Now," he yelled at James and Ventura.

Shane got to his feet and pushed James ahead of him before stomping on the back of the Hound's head and breaking its neck. Ventura led the charge to the back door through which he'd entered the house only moments earlier, with James behind him. Shane rushed after them, the two Hounds from the front of the house bounding down the hall over the bodies of the dead Harvesters.

Shane slipped his hand into his pocket, grasping for his iron rings as he followed the other two men outside. He turned in the doorway and ducked, bringing his fist up into the jaw of the nearest Hound only a pace behind him.

Iron met spectral flesh, and the ghost vanished, clearing a path for the second Hound. Shane swung his left fist and clipped the creature on the side of the head with a second ring, sending it back where it came from.

Ventura and James had stopped running in the darkness in front of him. With the Hounds temporarily removed, Shane focused on the others.

He swore out loud. Ventura and James were almost back-to-back in the middle of the large, empty yard. James had spent some time landscaping, and there were a few apple trees and raspberry bushes along one fence. A Hound stalked between the trees toward the living men.

More Hounds encircled the trio, coming to the yard from all sides. Shane counted at least a dozen. Another appeared in the house, ambling toward the back door and the yard where Shane and the others waited.

"I can't fight this many," Shane said, backing up to Ventura and James.

"This is Ventura, I need a location confirmation and an extraction team, and I need it now," the agent said, talking into a radio handset. Static crackled, and a voice replied a second later.

"Sixty seconds to target," it said.

"Back door. It's going to be ugly," Ventura said, putting the radio back in a holster on his belt. "We need to get to the road."

He pointed to the edge of James' property and the street that ran alongside it. Five Hounds were lined up between them and the road, closing in slowly like wolves surrounding their prey.

"You brought backup?" Shane asked.

"Harvesters are real-enough threats," Ventura explained. "Mr. Moran is the target of a doomsday cult, as far as my report indicates."

"How do we get to the street?" James asked.

Ventura pulled a length of metal from the holster next to his gun and handed it to James, retrieving another from the other side. The iron bars were long and thin, and he'd attached a leather loop on one end to ensure a grip. If nothing else, Ventura was prepared.

"Don't have anything else," the agent said to Shane.

"Not a problem," Shane replied, showing the rings on either hand. "You go first; I'll watch your backs."

Ventura didn't hesitate before running at the nearest of the Hounds. He had slipped his hand through the leather loop on his iron baton and swung like he was a horror movie slasher, bringing the metal down hard on the ghost's head.

James was only a step behind him, using the baton he held more like a rapier than a machete, stabbing it into the face of another Hound and returning it to wherever its haunted item awaited.

Shane kept his back to the two men but followed them, hands balled into fists watching the greater group of Hounds move toward him. The one from the house made the first move, taking a quick run before jumping at him with its hands extended.

He backhanded the Hound, clipping its shoulder with a ring, and then followed through as a second Hound came at him from the opposite direction.

The two that he originally dismissed had already rejoined the group. Shane guessed they were being housed in the van Ventura had seen out front, so the time difference between the iron banishing them and their return was less than a minute. It was a bad way to make progress, but it was better than nothing.

"Ryan, we're clear," Ventura shouted.

Shane looked over his shoulder and saw Ventura and James scaling the fence and heading toward the street. The way was clear, but more Hounds already circled the house to cut them off from the road.

A Hound jumped from the roof, catching Shane by surprise, and knocking him down, while the one that came through the apple trees attacked him from the front.

Shane's foot hit the second ghost in the head, and he felt something crunch in its face. The rooftop Hound was missing its lower jaw, but it leaned in as though trying to bite him anyway. Shane's fist hit it in the throat, and it vanished mid-lunge.

He was on his feet in seconds and racing for the fence. Ahead of him, Ventura and James were taking out the same Hounds they had dismissed once already. A black van appeared on the street, rolling up quickly with the side door open.

Ventura looked back at Shane, maybe ten paces behind, and shouted for him to run.

CHAPTER 18

LOST AND FOUND

The black van came to a stop, and a man in a dark suit held the door open. Ventura and James ran for it, Ventura taking one last swipe at a Hound.

Shane was over the fence and running as fast as his legs would carry him. Half a dozen Hounds rounded the side of the house, and behind them, a man with a rifle took aim at the van.

Ventura's backup fired a round. He missed, as the Harvester ducked behind a tree in James' front yard to avoid the shot.

Ventura was first in the van. Shane caught up with James just as the Hounds reached them. The first of them jumped Shane from behind, tackling him into the van on top of Ventura.

The agent holding the door was knocked backward against the far wall. Ventura struck out with the iron baton, hitting the Hound, and causing it to vanish just as a second bounded inside, going for Ventura's wrist to stop his attack. Shane tried to hit the ghost, but another entered the van and forced him back down.

The space was too tight for a proper fight. Shane struggled to free his hands or do anything that would allow him to hit the Hound and dismiss it, but the ghost slammed him to the floor of the van again and again.

Hands like ice slipped under Shane's armpits and lifted him roughly, raising him to the ceiling and then slamming him down. He felt one of the rings slip off his fingers.

The driver of the van shouted something Shane couldn't make out. He elbowed the Hound attacking Ventura and then twisted his body to grab hold of the one attacking him.

Shane's thumb hooked into the ghost's empty eye socket. He closed his fist, holding on as tightly as he could, and brought the ghost's face down to the floor. He pounded the ghost on the side of the head with his other hand, realizing that the second ring was also lost somewhere in the back of the van.

There was little time to waste. With his thumb still lodged in the ghost's eye, Shane forced the ghost's head down to the van floor and slammed down with all his weight, pushing his hands together.

The ghost's head cracked and collapsed. The van shook as though it had been rear-ended, and Shane was tossed back as the ghost exploded.

The second Hound was also tossed aside. Ventura recovered quickly, smashing the iron baton against it, and clearing the space.

Shane cursed again and got to his feet. James had not made it into the vehicle. He scrambled to the door, but the rest of the Hounds were gone, as were the Harvesters. James Moran was nowhere to be seen.

"They got him," Shane said to Ventura, who was checking the pulse of the fallen agent.

Ventura banged on the wall of the van.

"White van; follow it!" he shouted.

"The hell did you do back there?" the driver shouted back. Shane could hear the engine clicking as the key turned. The Hound's destruction had disabled the vehicle.

Shane left without another word, running across the yard to the front of James' house. There was no sign of any white van, the Harvesters, or the Hounds. They had gotten their prize and fled during the confusion.

"Vermont," Ventura said, joining Shane on the lawn a moment later. "I got the plates of the van before I went in. Vermont. We'll run a trace, see who it's registered to."

"He was right beside me," Shane said sharply. "We were at the goddamn door."

"It's not your fault, Ryan," Ventura said.

Shane looked at the agent and sighed.

"Of course, it's not my fault. I didn't kidnap the man. It can still piss me off, though."

"Well, yeah. Come on. There's a field office nearby. The sooner we track that van, the sooner we can get James back."

The FBI van was out of commission and would need a tow. They took Ventura's car and drove twenty minutes to the nearest office, where no one except a janitor was working.

"FBI keeps banker's hours or something?" Shane asked.

"It's a small field office. Don't have someone here twenty-four seven."

Shane grunted as Ventura used his ID to buzz them into the building and led them to a computer. He logged in with his credentials while Shane watched over his shoulder. A quick search showed that the license plate was registered to somebody in the town of Middlebury.

"We know anyone in Middlebury?" Ventura asked.

"Not ringing a bell," Shane replied.

Ventura brought up some files about Deacon, leases and property tax filings, and looked for anything in Middlebury. There wasn't anything in Vermont at all.

"Anything for Talbot?" Shane asked.

Ventura repeated the search. Talbot had once owned a property in Vermont, but it was a shop in Brattleboro. Nothing rural and nothing secluded enough to hide an operation that must be killing people by the dozen.

"We've got this Middlebury address; we can look into that," Ventura said, not convinced it would lead them anywhere. Shane shook his head. He was sure the name and address belonged to a Harvester. They'd find nothing there.

"Try Lanthimos," Shane suggested. "Adrian or Adrianos."

"Lanthimos? All right," Ventura said.

He typed in the name and searched the results.

"A. Lanthimos," he said. "Twenty-five zero seven, route one-twenty-five, Ripton, Vermont."

Shane leaned in closer as Ventura opened a new window and typed the address into it. A map zoomed in on the address and Ventura hit a button, giving them a street view of the forest.

"That's it," he said.

"The woods. In the middle of nowhere."

Ventura rotated the image and then stopped, pointing at a blurry red image on a tree.

"What's that look like to you?"

"Flag of some kind," Shane replied. The picture was poor quality, and it was hard to tell. "I've seen hidden driveways in the woods marked like that, so you can see them from the road at night."

Ventura switched back to the file from which he'd got the address and read through it.

"How old was Lanthimos?" he asked.

"Thirties?" Shane said. "Forties, maybe. Why?"

"There's a filing for a permit here under his name. Plumbing and electrical installations filed with Addison County. And it's not recent."

"How far is this from the diner where those guys that came for James had been?"

"Diner was in Bethel, just a few miles up the road," Ventura said. "This is our location. This is Mr. Shadow."

"Maybe," Shane agreed. It was a good lead; he wouldn't argue with that. But they had already lost at least an hour on the Harvesters. If this was wrong, James had almost no hope of surviving.

"I've got some gear in my trunk. I think we should head out now, get the lay of the land, and proceed once we have an idea of what we're working with. I'll alert the Albany office. They cover everything in Vermont, and I'll call them in for backup if we need something. I'll keep a team on reserve in Middlebury just in case."

"Just in case, huh?" Shane said. "Speaking of… those guys who rolled up for the rescue, what'd you tell them about what happened to their van?"

"Cult must have disabled it," Ventura said with a shrug.

"The doomsday cult," Shane clarified.

"That's the one. You ready?" the agent asked. Shane looked at the image on the computer again. Vermont forest. He hadn't had a lot of good times with ghosts in Vermont forests. He had a feeling this would be worse.

Shane waited out front, having a smoke by the car while Ventura got in touch with the Albany field office. Once everything was set, the agent unlocked the trunk of his vehicle and opened it.

The last time Shane went to battle with ghosts at Ventura's side, the agent had surprised him with the amount of gear that he had on hand. It looked like he had improved on his selection for this time around.

Being unable to physically fight spirits, a lot of what Ventura focused on was defensive gear. He had lightweight armor that was adorned with thin strips of iron, a sort of poor man's version of plate armor. The coverage across the arms, chest, and back was enough that any ghost trying to grab him would send it back to its haunted item. The armor was matched with a pair of fingerless gloves into which he'd sewn a set of rudimentary iron knuckles.

Offensive weapons consisted mostly of a variety of iron bars and batons. There were actual iron knuckles, as well as a telescoping baton— an iron bar that might as well have been a baseball bat—and then smaller, more maneuverable pieces.

"Grab a weapon," Ventura offered.

"Got these from the van," Shane told him, holding up the rings he'd lost earlier.

Ventura tossed him a small bag, which Shane caught and inspected closely. A thin zipper at the top held in a handful of iron shavings. Shane slipped the bag into his pocket and then took another one as Ventura loaded his pockets with several bags. In a pinch, the iron shavings were a quick way out of a sticky situation.

Shane glanced at the rest of the items in the trunk, and after a moment of consideration, took a thin telescoping baton that reminded him of a radio antenna. It was not the sort of thing he'd use to attack a living person, but it would be easy to wield against a spirit.

They hit the road shortly thereafter, with Ventura following GPS directions. They traveled down rural roads in darkness. At some point, Shane realized he'd fallen asleep. It had been a couple of days since he'd had any rest. When he opened his eyes, two hours had passed, and Ventura was slowing the vehicle.

Outside of the car was nothing but black forest. The headlights showed more of the same on either side, but the GPS voice assured them that they were approaching their destination on the right.

The men scanned the trees and saw nothing even as the GPS announced that they had reached their destination. Ventura drove slowly for another few yards before stopping the car, looking back over his shoulder at the red glow of the brake lights on the trees behind them.

"I didn't see it," he said.

"Keep going for a little bit," Shane suggested.

They moved at a snail's pace, scanning the trees until Shane caught sight of a flash of color.

"There," he said, pointing ahead.

The faded red flag was still tied to a tree, partially obscured by a branch thick with fat, green leaves. The car crawled along the empty stretch of road and then stopped. To their right, hidden among the trees, was a driveway that vanished into the woods.

Most of the path was overgrown, but the distinct runnels dug into the dirt from tires were there for those who knew where to look. The marks were fresh and well-used, even if weeds grew strong on either side and in the gap between. They camouflaged it well for anyone who was just passing at a regular speed.

Shane saw nothing in the woods. The mostly hidden path vanished into the trees and shadows. Whatever awaited them had been built far from the road, and probably would have remained a secret even in broad daylight.

Ventura backed up slightly and then turned, heading down the bumpy, uneven path through the trees. He turned off the headlights and kept the pace unbearably slow as he navigated by the nearly nonexistent light of the moon.

The road was relatively straight for a long distance, and then it curved to the left. Ventura kept the lights off, doing his best to follow the path without alerting anyone to their presence. They had traveled for nearly ten minutes when the woods thinned out and they emerged into a huge clearing.

"That's got to be the place," Ventura said, stopping the car.

To their left was a massive, dark house that rose nearly even with the treetops. Three vehicles were parked out front, including the white van.

Ventura put the car in reverse and backed up quietly to the cover of the forest. He took them as far back as the curve and then rolled right off the path into a thicket of ferns and saplings, running over the small plants before he stopped.

"We get separated, we meet back here," Ventura said.

They worked together, dragging branches and deadfall to cover the car. It would have been poor camouflage in the daytime, but the car was near-invisible in the dark.

"You ready?" Ventura asked when they were finished.

Shane stood at the edge of the dirt road, his jaw tense and nostrils flared. A breeze filtered through the trees, and on it came a familiar scent. Corpses were nearby. Rotting meat. And by the stench of it, there was a lot.

"Yeah. Let's go."

CHAPTER 19

HOUSE OF A THOUSAND CORPSES

Shane and Ventura stayed behind the tree line and made their way closer to the house, out of sight should anyone be watching from the windows. The house looked like no one had used it in decades.

Parts of the exterior wall were overgrown with vines and moss. The left side of the roof sagged to the point that it looked like it could collapse any day.

The shingles were clogged with detritus, old leaves, and twigs, and the eaves seemed to overflow with them as well. It looked like it was on the verge of collapsing under its weight and being overtaken by nature. Still, the vehicles out front meant at least some of the house was usable, and the Harvesters were inside.

The smell in the air grew stronger as Shane and Ventura got closer to the house. Shane had smelled death many times, but this was something else. He had been in slaughterhouses that didn't have a stench quite so pungent. What he smelled was not fresh, nor was it small.

The two men circled the property to the rear. At the back, a glass-encased sunroom had collapsed. The window panels that remained were dark and murky, covered with years of dirt, water residue, and mildew.

Judging from the weeds and overgrowth, the back of the house was used even less often than the front, but a path was worn from the forest to a door. Someone traveled, if not frequently, between the house and the dark forest beyond.

Shane grabbed Ventura's arm and stopped him from walking when he caught sight of movement among the weeds. They crouched next to a tree and watched as a Hound wandered leisurely along the rear of the house. It covered the length of the building, turned once it reached the far wall, and circled to the front.

"Guard?" Ventura guessed.

"Looks like," Shane said.

The slow and even pace made it seem like the Hound was following a routine it was used to. It could circle the house endlessly and would make short work of most trespassers, should anyone stumble on the property.

The men stayed still in the woods and waited. It took the Hound barely two minutes to return from around the front, circling the side closest to where they were hidden, and following in its footsteps around the back of the house in an endless loop.

"I don't see any other guards," Shane said.

"One's enough," Ventura responded.

He wasn't wrong. The guard Hound was larger than most of the others Shane had seen. The ones he had seen with Beatrix were smaller, and in some cases even frail. But the past several, since the attack on James, had been in much better shape. The spirits had been born from living bodies that were strong and athletic.

Something had changed in the process. With a hit-and-miss approach to making ghosts, Shadow would have had to take what she could get. But now, they looked handpicked, intimidating, and streamlined.

The potential answer was right there, though Shane did not want to voice it. The obvious explanation was that Shadow had learned how to make a ghost. Not just by chance, but accurately and definitively with each attempt. If that was true, she could curate the exact ghost she wanted every time.

Using a skill like that simply for a body type was foolish. If anything, it was to Shane's benefit that Shadow focused only on physical attributes. An athletic ghost was not much more intimidating or harder to deal with than an out-of-shape one. The muscles were technically no longer even real.

More concerning was what would happen if Shadow began to think about what this potential ability meant. If she could turn anyone into a ghost, then it was a simple matter of finding the worst people. The physical attributes didn't matter; it was the mind that transferred when someone died. If she harvested the worst people—serial killers and other maniacs—the chaos would be endless.

They waited for the Hound to reach the end of the property again before they continued scouting behind the house. The forest encroached much closer at the back than at the front, and as they took the corner from the side to the rear, the smell of death became even stronger.

"It's down there," Ventura said as they reached the path worn through the weeds into the woods at the rear of the house. The path continued through the trees, away from the house, and into the darkness.

Shane nodded and followed the footpath. It was meandering and uneven, a trail worn by feet but not created by tools. It was something that had been walked many times, the path of least resistance through the trees.

Ventura covered his face before the path reached a small clearing. Shane followed suit once the trees gave way, and the path came to its natural end.

A pit, either dug mechanically or some natural depression, took up most of the clearing. The poor light made it hard to see the fine details, and that was something of a blessing. Shane could see enough without it.

The pit was filled with bodies. A mass grave the likes of which he'd never seen. Animals growled at their presence. Raccoons, skunks, foxes, and a few night birds protested their arrival, but they only fled near the path's entrances.

In the dark, Shane heard the sounds of nature feasting. Not just the larger animals, but insects and larvae. The mass of bodies was so great that it had drawn every carrion eater it could.

"Jesus Christ," Ventura whispered.

It was impossible to tell how deep the pit was or how long Shadow had used it. Shane could only think of the date on the permits. She'd been there for decades.

The freshest bodies, though they didn't quite meet that definition, sat on top of the pile. Shane could make out faces, or the lack thereof. Flesh carved down to bone, the brutal masks each Hound was given. The bodies were bloated and broken. Some were pale and bloodless; others were purple or red or nearly black with rot.

There had to be hundreds. Shane had not even seen so much concentrated death in war zones. It was hard to imagine that so many people had gone missing, and many lives were taken, and no one had stopped it.

Shane remembered something Ventura had told him about the staggering number of people who go missing each year in America. Thousands of them would never be seen again, either dead or alive.

Shadow had found a way to exploit those numbers. The missing and the dead were just statistics, numbers on a page that made people feel bad about what was happening, even when they had no practical solution. How could anyone have stopped what Shane was looking at? No one would have even believed it. *He* could barely believe it.

"There are parts missing," Ventura said.

Shane looked toward where the other man indicated, his eyes falling on a headless body. An animal could have taken it. The rot was so severe, it would have been easy enough to just pull away. But the more Shane looked, the more he realized that parts were missing from many corpses. Some were missing arms, some legs. In other places were just loose arms and legs that had been surgically removed judging by the cleanness of the cuts.

"Haunted items, maybe," Shane suggested.

A ghost could be bound to a skull or other body part. That was the easiest explanation. He was not sure he wanted to ponder what other reasons the Harvesters had for keeping pieces of Shadow's victims. Something came to mind, though.

"You believe that?" Ventura asked.

"No," Shane said honestly.

The heads, perhaps, but the other parts were less likely. Torturing someone to the point that they would return as a Hound was not a fast process. Even if Shadow had found a way to guarantee that a person would return as a ghost, they still needed to create the monster first. That was a time investment. They needed to keep the body alive for days or weeks to get the desired results. That meant they needed to feed their victims.

Shane listened to the animals feasting on the corpses and was reminded of a conversation he had with Beatrix. She had broken into his home and held him at gunpoint just before she died. She had seemed unhinged, and the way she spoke was erratic and confusing. However, she had asked him if he had ever tasted human flesh. It had seemed like a crazy question that came out of nowhere. Now, it seemed much less random.

"I have to call this in," Ventura said. "I can't sit on this."

"We need to get into that house," Shane said.

"We will. But come on, Ryan. Look at this. I want feet on the ground now. I need agents here yesterday."

Shane understood Ventura's point of view. It was in Shane's nature to handle problems like this on his own, but Ventura was not playing the same game. This was a job to him. This was hundreds of unsolved crimes piled up at his feet.

Each of those corpses had once been a missing person. Each of them probably had friends and family who wondered where they had gone, and who were waiting for answers. Some of them had been waiting for decades. It was not Shane's place to keep the truth from anyone, even for just another few minutes.

Ventura pulled out his phone and made a quick call. He was whispering, trying to ensure that the Hound did not hear if it passed on its rounds. He gave the person on the other end of the phone the GPS coordinates of the house and then hung up.

"Cavalry is on the way, but it will take some time. We can still find James."

"We need to make sure none of the Harvesters get out of here. Shadow's been mobile in the past; she's not above running. They can't take anything from this building," Shane said. He didn't say what he meant, but Ventura understood the meaning. No one was going to leave alive.

"Not going to get an argument from me," the agent said, looking into the pit. He didn't plan to make arrests. The Harvesters had lost that courtesy.

"We're on the clock now, so let's get moving," Shane said, turning his back on the atrocity in the pit.

They made their way back up the path toward the house and then crouched among the trees, waiting for the Hound guard to reappear. When the disfigured ghost came back into view, Ventura split from Shane and stood in the center of the path. He whistled softly, drawing the ghost's attention.

Soundlessly, the Hound burst into a run straight into the trees toward Ventura. The FBI agent ran back toward the pit, leading the Hound away from the house and out of sight.

Shane ran after it once it was beyond the trees. The Hound only realized it was being chased when Shane tackled it. His attack was swift and brutal; they had no time for anything more.

The Hound landed face-down and Shane gave it no chance to recover. He scrambled up the spirit's body, twisted its head to the left, and then slammed his elbow into its temple, fracturing the ghostly skull. A second blow and the Hound burst, knocking Shane into the trees.

"You good?" Ventura asked, coming to his aid, and helping him up.

"Delightful," Shane said, dusting himself off. "Let's go kill some Harvesters."

CHAPTER 20
DEATH COMES FOR US ALL

Shane and Ventura waited at the edge of the forest. It had only taken the Hound a few minutes to circle the house on its patrol. They waited out what would have been a full cycle and neither saw nor heard anything. If anyone was monitoring the Hound, they would have come looking for it by then.

They followed the worn foot trail from the edge of the forest to the rear of the house. The back door had been used to extricate the bodies, and it was not locked. Shane doubted anyone in the house was concerned about break-ins.

Shane entered first with Ventura behind him. The house was dark, and the door led into a kitchen that smelled worse than the pit from which they had just come. At least the pit full of corpses was in the open air. The kitchen was sealed, humid, and lacked airflow.

The counters and floors were covered in blood. It looked like no one had ever cleaned it, and Shane couldn't imagine who could work in those conditions.

Flies buzzed about them when they entered, disturbed by the faint light and movement of the open door. The darkness kept them mostly docile, but they swarmed when the men entered.

The sound of buzzing wings and squirming larvae was like white noise, a constant wet droning in the background. Shane ignored it and focused on the path ahead. Two doors led from the kitchen, and he chose the nearest one, a straight shot from the back door to another wooden door with a gore-stained door knob a few paces away.

The door was also unlocked, and it opened easily. They left the kitchen and found themselves in a hallway that traveled left and right away from the kitchen to parts unknown.

Neither direction showed anything of interest nor seemed like a better choice than the other. Shane did not think it was wise to split up, knowing that there were others in the house. They'd have better chances of overcoming them together.

Shane turned left, though nothing drew him in that direction. Ventura followed without question, an iron baton drawn and ready. They walked softly and slowly, but the house was old, and the wood rot had spread from the outside to the inside.

It was impossible to avoid creaking the floor now and then. Each step that caused the wood to groan made Shane curse internally. His instinct was to stand still and wait it out, but he kept moving instead, not wanting to wait to be attacked.

He opened doors as they went, searching rooms that looked like they had not been used in many years. Some were piled with trash, broken furniture, and old food containers. Others were almost empty. One room near the front of the house with a big, bay window looking out onto the parking area actively grew small plants from seeds that had blown in through the broken glass.

Shane took another left down a nearly identical hallway and stopped when he opened the door and was met by even more rotten stench. Instead of a room, a set of stone steps led down into a dark basement, with a faint flicker of light somewhere in the distance.

There was more to the smell that came from the basement than what they had encountered in the kitchen. The smell of dampness and mildew was there, but a layer of human waste and sweat was mixed in. Not the smells of death, but the smells of life, however unpleasant.

Shane looked at Ventura, and the other man nodded. Not a word was exchanged between them before Shane started down the steps. The stone under his feet was slick, and he moved slowly, but at least it afforded him silence.

Shane was met at the bottom of the stairs by a large, circular stone room. It looked more like a dungeon than a basement of a house. Multiple hallways led away from the center room like the basement was a wheel with the stairs in the hub and spokes going off in every direction.

There were dim lights down several of the halls. Shane counted eight passageways spread evenly around the room.

A muffled scream caused Shane to freeze and jerk his head to the left toward what seemed like the source. He saw nothing down the passageway but a light in the distance. The scream echoed off the walls, but it sounded either very far away or very muffled. Another one followed, but not from the same voice or direction.

Ventura pointed to the passage directly behind the stairs. The hallway was wider than the others, and the lighting was brighter. Shane saw doors set into the stone walls at least as far as the curve in the hall several yards in.

They headed down the hallway as quickly as they dared. The source of the dim lights seemed to be nearly invisible sconces behind bricks in the wall. The lighting appeared to be electrical, but the bulbs were so dim they provided just enough illumination to know there was a hallway.

Shane stopped at a bulky, old wooden door with a thick metal handle. He tried to pull it open, but it was locked. Across the hall was an identical door that was also locked. Shane thought he heard a faint moan, but it was hard to say for sure.

He had no way of knowing if Shadow had moved into the house after it was built or if the ghost had intentionally designed it. In any event, the basement was built to hold and hurt people. The doors were cell doors meant to hold someone securely on the other side. This was where Shadow's victims were kept. This was where the Hounds were created.

The two men traveled deeper into the basement. The doors were evenly spaced, even as the hall curved and wound deeper into the ground. Some of the rooms were silent, but Shane heard weeping and moaning from some. He heard muted voices speaking in others, people talking to themselves or begging for help.

They had passed nearly a dozen rooms with more ahead when Ventura stopped.

"Eight hallways," he whispered. "Twenty rooms in each? Maybe more?"

Shane nodded. He could do the math. If all the rooms were full, if Shadow was creating new Hounds in each one, she was assembling an army.

The curve in the hallway evened out, and Shane saw a dead end. Only a short distance more and everything came to an abrupt stop against the flat, stone wall. Just before the dead end, however, was a thin, stone ridge on the left side of the passage, what looked like a doorway. None of the other doors had that feature; the doors were simply recessed into the wall. This was new.

Shane gestured for Ventura to be cautious and pointed out the door frame before taking the lead. The agent followed as they hugged the wall to stay out of sight and approached silently.

With his back to the wall, Shane turned to his left and peered around the corner. It was another doorway as he suspected, but different from the others. The door was wider, and it was also open. Shane was at eye level with the hinges and peered through the crack between the edge of the door and the frame from which it hung.

The room inside was lit slightly better than the hallway, but not by much. A single candle burned atop a small table. A man sat on the other side of it, his head down as he wrote in a small notebook.

The man was older than Shane, his hair white and his face heavily lined. He scribbled notes quickly and sometimes paused to mumble to himself before writing something else.

Shane gestured to Ventura again and indicated he was going to enter. Ventura followed his lead, and they moved quietly into the room so as not to disturb the man.

Ventura's gun clicked as he pulled back the hammer, drawing the attention of the older man and causing him to look up. His eyes widened in surprise, but he calmed soon enough and remained seated, resting his pen down on the notebook.

"Sorry to interrupt your homework," Shane said. "Where's James Moran?"

"He's indisposed at the moment," the man replied.

"I can start by breaking your fingers if you like," Shane said.

The man shook his head.

"I'd rather you don't," he said.

"Then try again. James Moran."

"He's in a cell," the man said. "He's unharmed so far."

"Good," Shane said. "Who are you?"

"Roy."

"Roy, I'm going to assume you're not an idiot, so when I ask you a question, I'm going to need you to give me the answer you know I want, not something stupid."

Roy nodded.

"The Harvesters call me the Houndmaster. I'm just here to do a job."

"A job," Ventura repeated.

"You murder people, then," Shane said at the same time.

"I curate spirits," Roy corrected. "It is a refined process, and yes, people die. I haven't killed any of the recent subjects; I only facilitate the process. Perhaps not a significant legal distinction, but worth noting."

"I bet you think so," Shane said. "You work for Mr. Shadow?"

"I do," Roy confirmed.

"So, you're the one who figured out how to make them, not Shadow? How to ensure someone comes back?"

Roy smiled and lifted his notebook.

"Yes! I've been working on this for years. You must understand what a delicate process it is to force a spirit's creation. The prevailing wisdom for the longest time was that it was impossible. But everyone I spoke to acknowledged that a spirit was more likely to be born from trauma, which indicated there was a process by which they were forged. It was not an easy path to understanding, I assure you."

Roy spoke with excited reverence. It was like listening to somebody getting into a hobby that you knew nothing about, explaining the intricacies of it with the loving devotion only a true hobbyist could have. Except in this case, he was talking about murdering people and using their pain as a jump-off point for creating a ghost.

"Do you have any idea how crazy you sound?" Shane asked.

Roy scoffed dismissively.

"To some, I have no doubt. But I know who you are, Shane Ryan. I spoke at length about you with Beatrix. You are like her! You understand this world better than most. Surely, you appreciate what this means. To customize a spirit, to ensure the return of the dead? This could change the world. Imagine if we could offer this to people. They'd never have to lose their loved ones."

"Jesus, he thinks he's a humanitarian," Ventura said.

"I *am* a humanitarian," Roy said. "Is there anything more human than the soul? I cultivate that. The pure essence of mankind, the true self. I can distill that and make it real for anyone. Imagine never having to be afraid of what waits beyond, knowing you can stay for eternity with those you love. Not a short, paltry, mortal lifespan, but for all time."

"At the cost of what? A month or two of torture in a dungeon?" Shane said.

Roy shook his head.

"It doesn't have to be like that. The Hounds are the most unique creatures I have seen. But the trauma need not be this severe to produce a spirit. I'm confident I can fine-tune the process. I can find the point at which crossover occurs and do so without extensive disfigurement."

"Just mild torture, then. I'm sure customers will line up around the block to let you brutalize grandma so they can harvest her ghost and keep her in the closet until Christmastime," Shane said.

"A crass assessment of what I have achieved here, Mr. Ryan."

"James Moran. And Mr. Shadow. Now," Shane said. "Before I get really crass."

CHAPTER 21
THE DEADMAKER

"In a lot of ways, you are responsible for this, Mr. Ryan," Roy said.

"That a fact?"

"It is. Had you not destroyed the earlier Hounds that Beatrix took with her, I would not have been as pressed to create new ones. You backed me into a corner, and that pressure helped me refine the technique I'm using now."

"Isn't that something? Take me to James Moran. Now."

Roy nodded and slowly got up from his seat.

"How did you end up here with Mr. Shadow?" Ventura asked.

"Dumb luck," Roy answered. "I never knew Mr. Shadow or Beatrix before I was hired. I spent most of my life hunting spirits, trapping them, and studying them. I wanted to learn everything I could. The problem, as I'm sure you know, is that there's no school for this sort of thing. Most people have no idea that spirits exist. Many who believe in them just believe in fairy tales and movies. And even those who have seen them have not studied them. They don't know the nature of what they are and how they're formed."

"You're a scholar?" Shane said.

"One of very few in the world. I learned about the Harvesters, about them taking customers on guided hunts, and made contact. Beatrix introduced me to Mr. Shadow when I explained that I could potentially help with their plans to create specific ghosts. Mr. Shadow was very eager to make that happen and has spent many years leaving the process to chance."

"You sound proud of yourself," Shane said.

"I am," Roy said. "Why wouldn't I be?"

"Because of that pit full of corpses in the woods out back," Shane answered. "How many bodies have you tossed in there?"

"I can't say off the top of my head," Roy answered. "But I keep notes on every subject. I believe, since I started work here, we are somewhere in the four-hundred-thirty range."

"Four hundred and thirty victims?" Ventura said.

"I prefer to call them *subjects*, but if you like, yes. There were more before me. I've only worked with Mr. Shadow for three years."

Shane was stunned to hear the man speak so plainly about killing so many. He had met monsters, living and dead, but none were so cavalier and unmoved by it. Roy sounded like he was discussing engines he'd rebuilt or tomatoes he'd picked. It meant nothing to him.

"Was it money? Some kind of grudge?" Ventura asked.

"What do you mean?"

"Why did you do it? Why kill so many people?"

"I needed to see if my theories were correct. To prove I could do it," he answered.

He offered a half-hearted shrug at the end and then smiled at both men. Shane had never wanted to punch someone in the face more. He wanted to knock out Roy's teeth and make him choke on them. It was only his need to find James that stayed his hand. Once he had what he needed, that would be another matter.

Before anyone said another word, a deafening gunshot reverberated off the stone walls. The bullet passed cleanly through Roy's forehead but exited messily out the back. In the light of the candle, Shane saw blood and brain matter splatter across the far wall.

Roy's eyes were still open, staring into Shane's as his legs gave out and he collapsed. Blood pooled around the dead man's head, and Ventura still had his arm extended, finger on the trigger, pointing the weapon at the space where Roy had just stood.

Ventura lowered the gun and looked at Shane, eyes wide, as the color drained from his face.

"I probably shouldn't have done that," he whispered.

"Nah, served him right," Shane said.

"I've never..." Ventura didn't finish the sentence. "I've shot at people before. Never killed anyone unprovoked, though. Never... murdered anyone."

"That wasn't murder," Shane said. "That was removing trash."

"He was unarmed."

"He was a monster."

"I can't... I don't have a right to kill someone for being a monster."

He stared into Shane's eyes, and Shane felt his jaw tighten. He reached out and took Ventura's shoulder, squeezing tighter than he needed to, producing just enough pain to get the man to focus.

"When we're done in here, when we've found James and taken care of Shadow, go walk into the woods out back. Look down into that pit at four hundred people and tell them that you didn't have the right to kill someone for being a monster."

Ventura sucked in a shaky breath, and Shane saw color returning to the man's face. He clenched his jaw and then nodded, and Shane patted him on the shoulder.

"You good?"

"No. But yes. Yeah. I'm good."

"Good. Let's go find—"

A burst of cold wind caressed Shane's back and arms, stopping him mid-sentence. The candle flame flickered out, and the room plunged into darkness. There was nothing more for the two of them to say. They rushed for the door, Ventura passing into the hallway first with Shane right behind. Something pulled at Shane's ankle, and he fell face-first onto the ground and was dragged back toward Roy's corpse.

The door to the room slammed with Ventura caught on the other side, and Shane was alone in the dark.

"Shane!" Ventura shouted, pounding on the door. Shane heard him struggle to open it.

"Go," Shane yelled. "Get James. Get everyone."

Ventura swore and slammed his fist against the door.

"Go!" Shane yelled again.

"I'll be back for you. Stay alive!"

Ventura left, and Shane was alone. Whatever had pulled his leg had let him go, and he made his way to a wall, putting his back against it as he got to his feet. He stood still in the dark, listening to muffled sounds from farther away in the basement. Seconds passed, and he made his way toward the door. Something back the way he had come, by Roy's corpse, scraped across the stone floor.

Another step toward the door, and another sound of something heavy moving on the floor. Shane stopped and looked around in the blackness. There was no light at all, nothing for his eyes to adjust to. There would be nothing to see until it wanted to be seen.

"I'm guessing this is Mr. Shadow," he said to the darkness. "Heard a lot about you over the past few days. Real sad story. Pathetic, really."

The darkness did not answer. Shane decided to press his luck.

"Even heard about who you used to be before you became *Mister* Shadow. Heard about you and the Talbot kids. You and Deacon. You had a thing for that lunatic, huh?"

A low rumble from the shadows was his answer. Not a growl, but not something moving, either. Shane smiled.

"That got a reaction. Why don't you tell me where you are, so we can have a proper conversation."

"I am… everywhere," a raspy voice replied. True to its word, the voice came at Shane from all sides. It was as though Shadow was whispering into his ear but also speaking from across the room.

"Very dramatic," Shane replied. "But that's your thing, huh? The Hounds and Beatrix and, hell, this dungeon. You're a bit over the top."

Instead of an answer, the room grew colder. Shane felt the temperature drop, the hair on his arm standing on end as goose flesh pebbled it, and the chill set into his bones.

"What are you planning for James Moran? He had nothing to do with what happened to Deacon, you know?"

Shane started toward the door again, walking slowly, carefully, in the dark, keeping his arms out so that he didn't walk into anything. At some point, the wall at his back slipped away from him, and even when he reached out, he could no longer feel it. He took small steps at first, and then longer strides. Soon, he realized he was not where he thought he was. He would have reached the door many paces earlier had he still been in the dungeon room.

Nothing was around Shane in any direction. He was lost in a vast, empty space. Mr. Shadow had created a dark illusion, an endless basement with no walls or doors. There was only black and cold.

The cold deepened, and he could not escape it. The temperature quickly plummeted. He felt frost build around his nose, freezing the moist air as he exhaled.

He continued walking, more to keep warm than to find something in the dark, waiting for Shadow to make a move. He didn't think she would be content to let him freeze to death in the dark, but she was willing to make him suffer. He just had to endure as much as he could.

Shane held himself close, his arms wrapped around his chest to seal in warmth as he walked. His teeth chattered involuntarily, and the cold stung his eyes and lungs as he breathed.

His hike through the frigid darkness seemed to go on and on. He had traveled at least a mile when he finally saw something. There was light ahead, barely noticeable and as dim as the light in the hallways.

The cold became biting all over. His fingers and toes had long since gone numb, and his head began to throb at his temples. The light source grew closer, and it motivated him to push onward.

Soon, it was clear what he was heading toward. Another candle, this one attached to a small holder on a wall. He had finally reached the edge of the room, of the illusion that Mr. Shadow had created for him.

Shane reached for the candle, seeking to warm himself with the small, weak flame. Before he could touch the wax, a hand in the darkness batted his away, and he was hit in the side by something large and fast-moving.

Shane fell to the ground and found himself looking up into the partially skinned face of a Hound. His hands and feet felt clumsy as he fought back, striking imprecise blows that were painful thanks to the cold.

He fended off attacks from the ghost's hands and its snapping, lipless jaws. Despite the numbness in his limbs, Shane struck several blows and caught the ghost by surprise.

They rolled together across the cold, stone floor until Shane was on top. He knelt on the ghost's shoulders and pushed his hands onto the thing's face, driving his palms down over the empty eye sockets. He was too numb to feel the pressure he applied, but he pushed as hard as he could. The bones around the empty sockets shattered and Shane felt his hands push through the crumbling matter and into its head.

When it exploded, the candle flame didn't flicker. Shane was thrust back against the wall, and he grunted as his back muscles seemed to contract as one. In the span of a heartbeat, he realized why the flame hadn't died. He needed it to see the second Hound.

The ghost ran at him, and Shane stayed low, not bothering to get to his feet. Instead, he pushed off the wall in a crouch and wrapped his arms around the Hound's left arm as it reached him, pulling the ghost to the ground and breaking off its arm at the shoulder as he rolled over it.

No noise escaped the Hound's mouth, nor did Shane expect a cry of pain or surprise. He was on the crippled monster's back as swiftly as he could get there, sliding his hands under the ghost's jaw and leaning back with all his weight until its head snapped off.

The flame shuddered this time, and the force of the Hound's destruction sent Shane in the opposite direction. He landed hard and was immediately set upon by a third Hound, which bit deeply enough into his shoulder to draw blood.

"So, it's like this, then," Shane said, jamming an elbow into the Hound's ribs and breaking several. "Let's go."

CHAPTER 22
TAUNTING SHADOWS

Shane landed face-down on the cold stone floor. Pain and numbness fought each other throughout his muscles and bones. It was a sensation he had never experienced and did not want to experience again. The ache seemed to penetrate every inch of him, but the numbness dulled it, making it at least ignorable.

He knew enough now to not try to rest. The fight was not over yet, and it would be foolish to think it was. Instead, he got to his knees in time to catch the fourth Hound.

His shoulder and nose were bleeding. He felt new bruises on top of old bruises across his body, even with the brutal cold numbing most of him. The blows from the ghost stung like fire, but it didn't slow him down. If anything, it fueled his desire to destroy them that much faster.

"This working out the way you planned?" Shane said to the darkness. He knew Mr. Shadow was listening and watching. The ghost was toying with him, and that was fine for now. He would destroy the Hounds and teach Mr. Shadow that losing them was much quicker than creating them.

Shane ducked low as the Hound approached. It leaned to meet him, but he was already rolling right, snapping the thing's neck as he did so. Its head twisted off when he hit the wall, and the spirit's body exploded. Shane missed the brunt of that one and was on his feet by the time the fifth ghost appeared.

He was breathing heavily, the cold air burning his throat and lungs, but he didn't care. He needed the air, and the chill kept him sharp and attentive.

The Hound ran straight at him with no finesse or hesitation. It met his foot, losing teeth in the process as Shane kicked it in the chin and knocked it backward.

He was on the Hound when it hit the floor, stomping its neck with one boot and then kicking the side of its head with the other. The head came loose and skidded across the floor for a second before the body came apart, thrusting Shane back once more.

Shane's back hit the wall next to the candle, but he remained upright. His hands were still balled into fists, and his eyes searched the darkness for his next attacker. One second became ten, and then soon, a minute had passed. Nothing else appeared from the shadows.

His breathing slowed, but he did not let his guard down. He was still stuck in the endless basement. There would be more. He didn't know how much longer he could keep going, but he would find out. If Mr. Shadow was going to win the fight, Shane would make her earn every inch of it.

"You would have been a good choice."

The voice came from everywhere once again, harsh and raspy. Some syllables felt like they were being spoken directly into Shane's ear while others sounded like they came from across the room, or right behind him, or even on the floor at his feet. No matter where he looked, however, there was nothing to see. Whatever Mr. Shadow was, wherever she was, there was nothing to see.

"For what?" Shane asked.

Nothing moved around him, and the dim candle burned steadily. Mr. Shadow seemed to have grown tired of losing Hounds.

"For my right hand," Shadow answered. "Had you been there with Benjamin and Brandy Jean, I would have chosen you."

Shane grunted. He would not have taken the job as easily as Beatrix had. But, to be fair, if he was a child in that situation, who was to say? Shane had grown up tormented by ghosts as Brandy Jean and her brother had. What if Vivienne had offered him a deal? If she had chosen to mentor him instead of trying to kill him?

"Why did you have to kill the boy and take the girl? What good did it do you?" Shane asked.

"It was not for good," Shadow answered, a hint of mockery in the raspy voice.

"You turned her into a confused, pathetic thing. Why?"

"I did not turn her into anything," Shadow said. "I needed arms. Legs. Nothing more. A pack beast. A tool. Whatever else she became was by her hand."

"She was barely coherent before she died," Shane said.

"If I had cared even an ounce for that girl, I might be sad," Shadow rasped. "But I did not. I needed her for what she could do and where she could go. That was all. Does that upset you? Are you broken-hearted for poor Brandy Jean Talbot?"

"I killed her. So no, I wouldn't say I'm choked up over it," Shane replied.

Mr. Shadow laughed. The candle flame shuddered with the sound, and the cold seemed to vibrate with the humming sounds of the laugh that came from all corners of the room.

"A mighty killer. I am in awe," the ghost mocked.

"What's the point of it all?" Shane asked, trying to keep the ghost on topic. "Beatrix was a means to an end. What's your end? What are the Harvesters for? The ghost hunts? What do you want?"

"I never wanted any of it," Shadow said, bored now. "Brandy Jean wanted to hunt. Wanted to destroy them. The Houndmaster asked for money. They needed supplies. None of it mattered to me."

"I don't believe you," Shane countered. "You wouldn't have spent years on these Hounds if nothing mattered. You wouldn't have come for James Moran."

The mirthful laughter came again, and the light dimmed.

"Oh yes. James Moran matters."

"Then it's always been about revenge. Revenge for a man dead for fifty years or more," Shane said.

"Exactly. Revenge for a man killed unjustly. Murdered in his home by a coward who couldn't even face his victim."

"Do you face your victims? The hundreds of dead in the forest? Do you look them in the eye and let them know why you're unjustly killing them?"

"This is the only justice!" Shadow hissed. The flame was nearly extinguished. "What more could these mortal lives want? I make them immortal."

"I'm not sure I understand your definition of immortal," Shane said.

"It is not for you to understand," Shadow said, back to the soft, raspy voice. "You are a living thing, caught in a living world. For now."

"James Moran didn't kill Deacon," Shane said.

"James Moran *did*," Shadow whispered. "This James, the older James, what difference does it make?"

"All the difference," Shane said. "It wasn't the older James Moran, either. Talbot sent the package that Deacon opened. He sent the ghost that killed him."

"I was there," Shadow hissed. "I saw with my eyes. Your lies cannot save Moran. Or yourself."

"What did you see?" Shane asked. "An envelope with a return address? You think he'd put his address on a killer ghost? You think he even cared enough about Deacon to want to kill him? Deacon was a nuisance. A pest. James' father never gave the man a second thought. He didn't care enough, just like you with Brandy Jean. He couldn't have cared less."

"I saw," Shadow insisted, anger coming into the voice now. "I know."

"You were duped. Taken in by Deacon's crazed paranoia."

"Moran hated him! He would have done anything to see Ezra dead."

"According to who? Deacon? Did you ever see them speak? Did you ever hear Moran threaten him? I bet you heard Deacon threaten plenty of people. He wrote them all down in his little files. All the people who wronged him. Funny how everyone was against him, don't you think?"

"You didn't know him," Shadow said flatly. "You don't know anything."

The flame from the candle went out, and Shane was plunged into darkness again. He laughed loudly and mockingly, standing blind and waiting for what came next.

"Fifty years you've been focused on a fool's errand, duped by a lazy trick. You let the real killer escape you for years, and when you finally finished him off, you sent someone else to do it on your behalf. Talbot made you into a fool."

"Talbot had nothing to do with it! He was there to save Deacon. He saved us all in the aftermath."

"Yes, of course," Shane said. "Brave Lucas Talbot, who conveniently showed up even though no one knew Deacon was in danger. Who salvaged all of Deacon's ghosts, the ones they argued about so often when the men were in business together. Who knew exactly what to take and when before closing Deacon in that lead vault and leaving him there forever."

"You know nothing," Shadow growled. "Ezra was never left in the vault."

"Oh, I'm sorry," Shane said. "You didn't know. His body was taken away. But his ghost was in the vault, sealed in by lead. He'd been there this whole time."

"Lies," Shadow whispered.

"His body was broken and bruised. And his face was almost peeled completely off, but not quite. Like someone didn't know for sure what they were doing. Must have been your first time, huh?"

The darkness around Shane howled, and cold buffeted against him. He stood his ground, squinting against the frozen wind that tore at him and seeped into his flesh.

"What a shame you didn't care about Brandy Jean," Shane shouted over the howling wind. "If only you had arms and legs to take you back to that vault now."

The wind died immediately as though a door had been closed. Light returned to the room from a new candle. The endless floor was gone, and Shane was back in the small room. Roy's body was still on the floor, and the candle he had lit on the desk burned warm and orange.

Shane could not see Mr. Shadow, and the door to the hallway was still closed.

"You can take me there," Shadow said, her voice coming from the farthest corner where the light would not touch.

"To the vault? To see Deacon?" Shane asked.

"Yes. Take me to him," she insisted.

"You need to release James," Shane said.

Shadow made a low, rumbling sound like a growl.

"After I have seen Ezra."

"Now, or I take you nowhere," Shane countered.

"I can turn both of you into Hounds and have one of the Harvesters take me there. I don't need you."

Shane shrugged off the threat.

"You could, but I don't think you want to. None of the Harvesters can do what I can."

"You overestimate your value, living man. I know the secret to crossing over now. I can turn anyone I choose into a ghost. I can scour the living from the whole world and replace them all with loyal servants. I can do anything."

"Except travel to Syracuse on your own and get into a lead vault."

Mr. Shadow growled again, a very soft sound that came from nowhere and everywhere at once.

"I know what I saw, living man. Take me to Ezra, and we will ask him who killed him. You will see the truth. Moran is to blame. He doesn't deserve to go free."

Shane rolled his eyes.

"You think Deacon has any idea what happened? The fool who opened the box and let his killer out? That's why Talbot did what he did. He knew you'd all be too stupid to figure it out."

Something moved in the corner, and Shane saw not a shape but an amorphous cluster of darkness. It peeled away from the corner, allowing the light to fill the space where it had been. There was no shape, no outline or form or anything. It was just darkness moving across the room.

"You have nothing for me. I will find another way to Ezra," Shadow said.

Shane laughed even as Hounds began to appear in the wake of the moving darkness, filling in the darkest spaces where they were just barely visible.

"You think this is a joke?" Shadow asked.

"Of course not. You're the joke," Shane said. "You think I found Deacon in that vault and just left him there?"

The air grew cold again, and the shadow stopped moving. The Hounds were frozen in place, some swaying hypnotically, all of them focused on Shane like cats watching a mouse.

"Where did you take him?"

"Take him?" He laughed again. "I didn't take him anywhere. When you abandoned him in that room with every bone in his body shattered and his face scraped off his skull, when you left him there for decades, he went mad. Utterly, incomprehensibly insane. The thing I found didn't have the mind of a man; it was an animal. And I put it down like one."

CHAPTER 23

IRON AND SHADOW

The cold hit Shane and felt like fire as he stumbled back against the wall. The pain was as intense and severe as anything Shane had ever felt. His eyes watered, and the moisture immediately froze into beads on his face.

He raised his arms to protect himself and turned his back, but there was no direction from which he could relieve himself of the assault. The cold rained from every direction. It was like being trapped in a vortex, a black hole where freezing temperatures were being pulled into him from every angle.

"Imagine how he felt," Shane shouted over the rush of the frigid wind that threatened to freeze him. "Imagine what he thought knowing you did that to him and then left him there forever."

He laughed loudly and obnoxiously. He let tears flow down his face and freeze in place as he barked the most mocking laughter he could toward the darkness.

The cold ended as quickly as it had begun. Shane felt numb all over, then felt a prickly pins-and-needles feeling take hold on every exposed bit of flesh as the normal temperature of the basement warmed him. He ignored it.

The formless dark, the amorphous thing that was Mr. Shadow came toward him. It didn't even seem like a solid thing, like any sort of being at all. It was just a place where the light could not touch, with no definite outline or form.

While Shane watched, the hazy darkness solidified and took on a sharper, more defined shape. Shadow came toward him, slowly binding together and forming a recognizable outline. He could see a head, arms, and legs, even if no features were present.

Shane's laughter died down, but there was still a smile on his face as Mr. Shadow came within arm's reach. The darkness slipped away. Shane saw the face now, and it was one he recognized.

The ghost was the same one from Jeffrey's illusion. The woman who had lamented Deacon's passing and cried over his nearly dead body. The one who had carved his face away with her fingernails in the hopes of forcing his ghost to be born from the trauma.

Even without the obscuring layer of darkness that she wore in the Mr. Shadow persona, Shane saw something different about her. Ghosts did not age or change the way a living person did. But they could still alter their appearance.

The ghost's hair was darker than the honey color Shane remembered from Jeffrey's illusion, though part of her was still scalped and wounded. Her face looked thinner, and Shane realized after a moment that it was more skeletal, as though the flesh had thinned and the bone beneath had pushed closer to the surface. It didn't alter what she looked like, it just made her seem more severe. It made her look more dead.

She stared at Shane. She was shorter than him and had to look up to see him. Her eyes were black on black, both the iris and the pupil too large for a normal eye. He saw only hate in those eyes, not that he cared. He was glad to have created such a response. He had made her feel something negative, something unwanted and punishing.

"You are a liar," she whispered, her voice like sandpaper.

They were so close that Shane could have taken her by the throat. He wanted to. He wanted to remove her head from her shoulders and end everything, but he needed to know where James Moran was. If she had left him with Harvesters or Hounds, he needed to know where he was and how to save him. But the moment that was done, she would be finished.

"You know I'm not. You know I saw the face you carved. Not as clean as these," Shane said, gesturing to the Hounds that lined the edges of the room. "No polish to the bone. No precision to the cuts. Hasty work."

"So," the ghost said softly. "You came here to die."

Her voice was almost gentle, and very low but restrained. Shane felt the hate, and now, a cold, building rage. Her path to the present made that much more sense. Her long, drawn-out revenge. She was cold fire. She let her anger simmer low and slow. Shane could only imagine what it took to make the ghost blow her top, to lose her composure in an instant rather than let it play out over decades as she had done. But he wanted to find out.

"I came here for my friend. Destroying you would be a nice addition, though. Do you want to know how I ended Deacon? Do you want to know what he said before he died a second time?"

Below them on the floor, Shane saw shadows swirling about like smoke. Her rage was building.

"He didn't say anything," Shane explained. "He couldn't speak. You left him as dumb as these Hounds, only less trained. I broke his skull like an overripe melon and put him out of his misery."

The shadows on the floor surged up between Shane and the ghost, blocking her like a curtain. The shape of the woman was gone, and now, Mr. Shadow rose to the ceiling and beyond, the darkness making the stone above them disappear and giving Shadow even more room to grow.

Mr. Shadow still bore the shape of a person in the vaguest sense. There were arms and the form of a head, though the latter had no facial features.

The corners of the room glowed with a silver and gray fire. It flickered and burned, alternating light and dark. The light it cast illuminated Mr. Shadow and made the nearly human wraith visible in a way it had not been before.

The Hounds stalked forward from among the flames. Mr. Shadow had brought five more into the room. They moved as one instead of taking their turns as the first group had. Shane had no hope of defeating them all at the same time, even if Mr. Shadow only stood by to watch. He wasn't sure he could even take on one more given how he felt, the numbness in his limbs, and the weakness in his muscles.

He plunged his hands awkwardly into his pockets. It was hard to force his fingers to do what he wanted, but they were slowly warming. He was gaining more dexterity and more precision with every moment. He just had to draw it out a little bit longer.

He felt the pressure of the iron rings in his pockets. That was not all he felt. He would give Mr. Shadow a run for her money. Ventura was still out there somewhere. Shane had to hope he was getting something done.

Shane forced the iron rings onto his fingers. If he could not destroy the Hounds, he could at least buy himself some time.

The closest of the deformed spirits jumped at him just as Shane pulled his hand from his pocket. No longer intent on grappling with and destroying the Hounds meant he could change his fighting style to one that was faster and more defensive.

The Hound reached for Shane, and he met his hand, fist for fist. The iron ring crunched against the ghost's swollen, malformed knuckles. It popped out of existence and vanished from the room.

Shane pivoted easily into his next attack, taking on the second Hound with a backhand that hit it in the elbow. Like the first, the Hound vanished in a blink as though it was never there.

A deep, resonant bellow erupted from Mr. Shadow as the remaining three Hounds came for Shane simultaneously. With his back to the wall, Shane lashed out, striking the first and most convenient bit of exposed flesh on each one.

The Hounds were not trained to fight; they were just average people whose minds were as broken as their bodies. They had instinct, and whatever Shadow had done to them to gain their loyalty through fear and pain motivated them to attack like animals. None could think strategically or understand what to avoid in a battle.

The three Hounds vanished one after the other as Shane's fists connected with each of them. He knew the victory would be short-lived. Wherever the Hounds were kept had to be in the basement. He had bought himself mere seconds and nothing more. But it was enough.

Mr. Shadow shrieked. It was the sound of rage, the tipping point Shane had hoped to reach. The ill-defined shadowy arms swept in his direction, and he could see that the hands had formed into real, clear appendages. Her fingernails were like knives, an improvement on what she'd used to skin Deacon. They were scalpel blades refined from darkness, glossy black and razor thin.

She swiped through the air, and Shane ducked to avoid the strike. Stone crumbled from the wall as her nails sheared through it. Chunks fell onto Shane as he darted away, avoiding a strike from her other hand that dug through the wall and then into the floor where Shane had been a moment earlier.

He scrambled toward the silver fire but shrank back when he realized it was more than just an illusion. No heat came from the flames, but they burned with an intense cold. It was the same chill that had blasted him earlier, intense and painful. He could not get past it without extinguishing it first.

Mr. Shadow's attacks were not as fluid as they could have been, nor even as graceful as the Hounds'. She was maintaining too many illusions at once, trying to do too much at the same time. The size of the room had been altered, her size had changed into something towering over ten feet, and the silver fire burning at the borders of the room had to be tapping her strength and focus. The result was her being too slow and too clumsy to keep up with Shane as he darted away from her blows.

The ghost soon realized the fault in her approach. The silver fire faded away, and the ceiling appeared above their heads once more as the ghost returned to normal size, though still cloaked in darkness. She began to move faster, the razor claws of shadow getting closer to their target.

Shane felt for the small bag in his pocket, the dense bundle he'd carried with him since the FBI field office stopover with Agent Ventura. He pulled it free and squeezed the bag, forcing it open.

"Think you'll have anything to say before I crush your skull later?" Shane asked. "Or will you just go out wailing like a trapped animal the way Deacon did?"

Shadow's enraged cry was deep and full of fury. Shane threw the bag of iron shavings at the dark center mass of Mr. Shadow's chest. The tiny fragments of metal spread like a cloud, peppering the ghost's body with an unavoidable rain of iron.

Shane was prepared to break for the door as soon as Shadow disappeared, and return to the hall to find Ventura and James. Only Shadow didn't disappear. The dark form shuddered and then nothing. Her haunted item had to be in the room with them. There was no place to which the iron could return her since they were already there.

Mr. Shadow laughed, and Shane swore.

CHAPTER 24

RUN FOR YOUR LIFE

Darkness enveloped Shane as though Mr. Shadow had exploded and became the entire room. It swallowed Shane whole, and there was nothing left for him to see. The candle flame was extinguished, and the floor and walls were gone. He felt like he was floating, weightless, and held up by the emptiness.

"I've kept men alive for months," Shadow whispered. Her voice was soft at his ear. He could feel her cold breath, but when he turned to face her, nothing was there, and the voice moved with him. "I can make you suffer like no man ever has."

"You think so?"

"I know the Houndmaster's secrets. How to stave off infection. How to feed you the liquified remains of the other Hounds through a tube. You'll beg for death. You'll promise me the world to end your suffering. And I won't."

Shane was going to reply but stopped. A sound in the darkness, muffled and far away, silenced him. He listened and heard it again, then again, three more times in quick succession, and he was positive that he was not hearing things. Someone was firing a gun.

"Hear that?" Shane said. "That's the sound of you losing. Losing the Harvesters, losing this house, losing everything."

He laughed again, a genuine laugh this time. The gunshots, faint and little more than soft pops reaching his ear, were too frequent to be from one man. Ventura's backup had arrived.

Mr. Shadows' growl of frustration was swift and bestial. The darkness surrounding Shane vanished and swirled around the center mass of the ghost as she stalked away from him toward the door.

"You'll never have another Hound," Shane said, coming after her. "Never have another servant to be your arms and legs in the world. You wasted all those years for nothing."

He chased her to the door, and an arm of massless darkness surged from her body and slammed into his chest. Shane was knocked backward and he gasped for air as he hit the ground, feeling the pain of the blow and the subsequent fall upon hitting the hard stone floor.

"Nothing more needs to happen," Mr. Shadow said from the door. "Except the death of James Moran."

She vanished through the wood of the door. Shane coughed as he sat up awkwardly, his ribs aching. The numbness from the cold had dissipated, and he felt his body again. The sensation was a blessing and a curse as he regained his dexterity but was now much more acutely aware of the cuts and bruises that seemed to cover every inch of him.

Shane got to his feet and rushed to the door. He tried the knob, but it was locked. He slammed his shoulder into it, but the door held fast. Shane tried again, putting his full weight behind the assault, slamming his shoulder again and again against the wood in the hopes of jarring it loose. The door held fast in the frame.

Frustrated, Shane turned back to the room. The candle on the table was still lit, and the Houndmaster's body was a short distance away. The light reflected off the pool of blood that had formed around the dead man's head.

Shane searched the dead man's pockets for anything useful. He found a cell phone and a keychain but nothing else that could have helped him.

He used the light from the cell phone to inspect the keys, sorting through a handful that could have been for anything. A car key was in the mix, and maybe a padlock key. He took the keychain to the door and tried each of them in the lock.

The third key Shane tried slid smoothly into the lock. It clicked softly when he turned it, allowing the heavy, wooden door to swing inward. The sound of gunfire in the hallway was much louder than it had been in the room. It was still muffled, and Shane wasn't sure it was in the house, but the rate of fire had increased, and the sound was unmistakable. There was a firefight somewhere, between the Harvesters and the FBI, he assumed.

Shane rushed down the hall, checking the doors that he passed, looking for James. He used the Houndmaster's keys to open the lock across the hall to find another man passed out on the floor, hooked up to IV fluids, with his legs broken.

A heart monitor showed that the man's blood pressure was very low, but he still had a pulse. There was no way Shane could help him out and find James so he left him there with the door unlocked so Ventura or his men would find him.

Room after room, Shane was met with the same scene to a greater or lesser degree. None of Mr. Shadows' victims had been skinned; Shane imagined that was the final touch before they were killed. But many had been tortured and brutalized beyond words. Some had ribs that were so badly fractured that the bones jutted from their chests. Others were curled into balls, their arms and legs little more than tubes full of shattered bone and bruised flesh.

Most of the would-be Hounds were hooked up to monitors and IV fluids. Some had feeding tubes, and the smell in the rooms indicated exactly what they were being fed. The stink of rotten meat, human waste, and sweat hung heavy in the air. Each room was a nightmare. All Shane could do was leave the doors unlocked and hope that Ventura's team would arrive in time to save some of them.

A few of the victims were newer; some were even conscious when Shane entered and begged him for help. He told them that people were coming, and they would soon be free, and that they just needed to hold on a little longer. He said it again and again, hoping it was true and that they could still be salvaged from the dungeon.

In truth, he couldn't imagine that some of the people he discovered had a hope of ever living a normal life again. Even if they could be saved, they would be crippled forever. Maybe they would forget what happened with time or find some way to come to terms with it. It would be an uphill battle for every one of them.

He had returned to the central hub of the basement dungeon and the stairs that led to the main floor. James was not in any of the rooms down the hall where Shane had found Mr. Shadow. He took the next spoke and searched through those rooms, again finding future Hounds in various stages of torture and suffering.

He heard someone running on the floor above him, and then another loud gunshot, the loudest he had heard so far. The sound was followed by the dull thump of a body hitting the floor. Someone had just been killed, but there was no way to know whether it was a Harvester or law enforcement.

The seconds were ticking by, and Shane was no closer to finding James. There were so many rooms to check, and they were all the same.

He returned to the central hub and made his way to the hallway that went in the opposite direction of the one where he'd found Mr. Shadow. It was the first one he looked at when he and Ventura came downstairs. A faint light came from somewhere at the end of the hall, and Shane went toward it.

Shane passed rooms this time, looking for something different. Mr. Shadow had something in mind for James; she wouldn't have kept him in a random cell. There had to be a place especially for him. He wasn't there to become a Hound; he was there to be murdered.

The hall curved just as the one he had been in, only this time it did not end in a mysterious, dark room. The hallway led to another set of stairs that led deeper into the earth.

The second staircase was formed from stones and cobbled together.

The steps were not even under Shane's feet as he made his way down.

Shane used the light from the Houndmaster's cell phone to see where he was going as he descended into the subbasement. The stone steps went down to a landing and then curved left and headed farther down.

He saw the floor at the base of the stairs. It was packed earth, not stone, and looked surprisingly dry given the dampness in the rest of the dungeon. As Shane made his way down, a Hound stepped out from the darkness. It was crouched on all fours, its limbs broken just like the others.

The left half of the Hound's face had been scraped clean. The eye socket was black and empty, and the skeletal teeth were exposed. The right side was as pale as the rest of the spirit but still adorned with flesh. A milky white eye looked up at Shane, and thin, peach-colored lips were closed tightly over half its mouth.

The cut that separated the hemispheres was placed perfectly down the center of the face, equidistant between the eyes and down the centerline of the nose, lips, and chin.

Shane was not looking to waste his time on another fight with one of Mr. Shadow's Hounds. He wondered where the rest of them were; the ones he had already banished with his iron rings. They could have been fighting above him, attacking Ventura and his men, who would be defenseless against them. All the more reason not to waste time worrying about them in the house. He needed Shadow. He needed to find James.

The sound of gunfire followed him down the stairs, louder now than it had ever been. The fight had moved into the house. Shane was not sure how many Harvesters were in the building, but they were holding their own against the FBI. If the Hounds were part of the fight, it was possible that whoever Ventura called in would not survive much longer. Their bullets would not harm ghosts, and most of the living wouldn't even be able to see them coming.

Shane ran down the steps, jumping from the second-to-last step as he dropped the light onto the dirt floor. The Hound parted its jaws, releasing a soft, breathy sound but nothing more. It tried to grab Shane out of the air, but his fist crushed into the fleshy side of its face, the iron ring hitting it in the ear. It vanished, and Shane hit the ground and rolled, getting quickly to his feet.

He retrieved the fallen cell phone and used it to light his path. The walls in the subbasement were the same cobbled bits of stone and brick that the stairs had been. The ceiling was low, just a few inches above Shane's head, and he saw no doors set into the walls.

The dirt floor, hard-packed as it was, showed no footprints. If the Harvesters ever came down here, they hadn't left any sign.

There was only one path forward from the stairs down the short, narrow hallway. The Hound had been left down there to guard something. Shane just hoped he'd made the right choice in abandoning his search of the dungeon cells.

In the darkness ahead of him, Shane heard a scream. There were no words, just a cry of pain, but Shane recognized the voice.

It was James Moran's.

CHAPTER 25
DEAD AND BURIED

Shane ran down the dark hallway. It curved slowly at first but then in a more pronounced way, and he realized he was following a spiral into the ground. The sound of gunfire behind him grew fainter until it was hard to tell if he heard anything at all.

The hallway came to an end at another wooden door. This one was only half-closed; no one had bothered to lock it. As Shane approached, another scream erupted from within. It sounded like James was biting back the pain, clenching his teeth to muffle his response, but no man could withstand torture and silence forever.

Shane pushed the door out of his way and entered a small room with a domed ceiling. James was on a table that had been tilted upright in the center of the room so that he was almost standing. His wrists and ankles were attached to it with leather straps, and his shirt had been cut away. Nothing else was in the room except a bucket and a small set of three drawers on wheels, the sort of thing someone might have in a home office. An unusually bright light in the center of the overhead dome illuminated everything.

Mr. Shadow stood before James, no longer in her amorphous, cloudy form. She was the woman again, half of her face and scalp shorn away, shadows swirling at her feet but nowhere else.

Her fingers all ended with those scalpel-like nails. The razor-thin blades danced across James' exposed flesh, and Shane saw she had already started her work, removing strips of skin from his chest and shoulders. Some were just slices, but others were as thick as a thumb, peeled down to the muscle and tossed into the bucket beside her. The blood ran freely down James' body, saturating his pants and dripping onto the dirt.

Shane's instinct was to attack. He wanted to fight Shadow, to destroy her once and for all. He could see, however, that James was badly injured. Numerous cuts had already been inflicted on him, and the wounds were very deep and bleeding openly. He didn't think his friend had time to waste.

Mr. Shadow was powerful and fighting her would not be quick. He couldn't risk letting James bleed out on the torture rack.

Shane reached into his pocket and retrieved the second bag of iron filings. He knew where Shadow would go now, and how much time they had to escape. They wouldn't be able to make it out without help. But he could get James down and moving.

Iron filings flew from Shane

s hand in an arc. He said nothing to announce his presence, and Mr. Shadow didn't even have time to acknowledge Shane's presence before the metal struck her dark form and returned her to the room on the far side of the dungeon.

"You still with me?" Shane asked, coming to James' side. The older man was breathing heavily, but he nodded.

"I may be a few ounces lighter," he said. "Nothing that won't grow back."

Shane set to work on the leather restraints that held him in place. He released James' right hand, allowing him to work on freeing his left while Shane took care of the ankle restraints.

"She'll be back fast; I didn't send her far," Shane explained.

"Agent Ventura?" James asked.

"Sounds like he's upstairs in a gunfight with the Harvesters. Exit is two flights up after this winding hallway, but we're not going to make it without a fight," Shane explained.

"I'm not going to be much good if it comes to that," James said.

Shane reached into his pocket and pulled out the last of the items he'd taken from Ventura's trunk. A thin, short piece of metal, no longer than a finger, with a rounded, iron knob on top. He handed it to James, who inspected it for a moment before pulling on the knob. The baton extended to a length just shy of fifteen inches or so.

"Interesting," James said.

"Make good use of it. There might be Hounds and—"

Shane stopped himself as shadows oozed into the doorway like oil spreading through water. He knew that Mr. Shadow would return quickly, and she had not disappointed. Now, she was blocking their only exit.

The iron worked well enough to send her back to her room, to whatever haunted item bound her to that place, but their progress would be slow if they only had a few minutes between each time they vanished her and her return. She would find a way to get around the iron soon enough. Whether that meant rushing them with Hounds or freezing them in place with the cold wind before they could get within striking distance, Shane couldn't say. She wouldn't allow them to leave so easily, though.

"You'll die now, living man," Shadow said softly. "Nothing elaborate. Nothing noteworthy or remarkable. A forgettable death for a man worth forgetting."

"Honeymoon's over, is it?" Shane replied.

He knew that Mr. Shadow's patience with him would eventually wear thin. It had been his intention. He wanted her to feel pressed, to lose the cool demeanor she pretended she had. He wanted her emotional and vulnerable.

Shane slipped his hand back into his pocket.

"Do you remember this?" Shane asked.

He pulled the small, wooden box from his pocket and held it up. Barely larger than a typical ring box and latched on three sides, it had been the thing Ezra Deacon had taken from the envelope that purportedly came from James Moran Jr., the thing that Lucas Talbot had sent his former business partner.

Shane pulled open the clasps on the box and threw it on the ground. The lid opened, and a pitted, cheap-looking ring inside rolled out, wobbling slightly before it fell on its side in front of Mr. Shadow.

The lights in the ceiling flickered, and in the brief, almost imperceptible moment of darkness, a figure appeared in the room between the living and the ghost. The spirit's back was to Shane, as it had been when he saw it in the illusion. The dirty white tank top hung loose over greasy blue jeans. There were sores and red rashes on the arms and broad shoulders.

Lanky, greasy hair hung over the ghost's face, and it turned to look at Shane. For the first time, Shane saw who it was, and he was briefly at a loss for words. He knew the face, impossible as it was. He had seen that ghost destroyed once already.

"Cassius?" he said.

The ghost had nearly killed Shane. He had gone toe-to-toe with Cassius several times, and the spirit had murdered at least a dozen people before Shane took it down in a fight between the ghost, himself, and Beatrix.

The ghost smirked, sores on his face oozing a clear liquid. In the doorway, Mr. Shadow pulled back. The darkness that swirled around her vanished, and she was revealed as herself once again, not hidden by the murk. Shane saw in her eyes that she recognized the ghost, remembering it from what had happened to Deacon. He thought he had seen hate before, but the look on Mr. Shadow's face was animosity unlike anything Shane had seen.

"You know my brother?" the ghost said. "Guess he's not dead enough yet."

Shadow stepped toward Cassius' brother with a finger extended, the end forged into a long, curved scalpel blade. He looked at her and grinned, cocking his head slightly to one side as she approached him.

"I know you," he said to her.

Shadow said nothing. She raised her hand and slashed toward the ghost of Cassius' brother. He caught her wrist effortlessly and held up her arm, his smile widening as he leaned down to look her in the eye.

"I remember you," he said, something close to joy in his voice. "You wept like a child when I tore that man to pieces."

She slashed at him with her other hand, cutting into the ghostly flesh of his chest but failing to wipe the smile from his face. He took her other wrist in his free hand and held her there with her arms spread wide as though he planned to split her in two.

"Was he your man?" the ghost asked.

Shadow writhed in his grip, but her struggle only amused him more. The two of them stood between Shane and the door, blocking the path to escape.

"Did you love him?" the ghost mused. "Did it break your heart to see what I did to him?"

His tone was mocking, but Shadow was not taking the bait. Shane did not know what sort of spirit Cassius' brother was, but he understood that he was not the sort to turn your back on. Talbot had sent one monster to destroy his partner.

Instead of answering, Shadow twisted in the ghost's grip, bending her arms, and spinning backward as she kicked her attacker in the face, knocking teeth from his mouth.

The bigger ghost growled angrily and released his grip. Shadow leaped at him, knife fingers digging into his dead flesh again and again. He fell back at Shane's feet with Mr. Shadow attacking him like a wild animal.

Cassius' brother was at least a foot taller than Mr. Shadow, and if they were both still alive, he would have been at least a hundred pounds heavier, but it didn't matter now that they were dead. The razor-sharp fingers sliced through his flesh like butter. She peeled chunks off him, and he raged against her, grabbing her face in his hand and slamming her head on the ground next to them.

She dug her hands into his guts, cutting out parts of his insides. Though her fighting style was brutal, it was not entirely effective against someone who was already dead. The ghost didn't need his intestines to destroy her, but she was too focused on injuries that would have hurt the living and not ones to incapacitate a spirit.

The bigger ghost grabbed her by the wrist once more as she came for his face. He was not taunting her this time, and not interested in an emotional response. Instead, he took her elbow in his other hand and snapped her arm over his leg, splintering the bone and breaking off her hand. He threw it toward the bucket in which she had been tossing pieces of James, but it vanished before it landed.

Shane made a play for the door, but Mr. Shadow reached for it with her handless arm. The swirling shadows around her feet snaked up her body and extended from the broken appendage, slamming the door shut and sealing it behind shadows so that it couldn't even be seen.

The distraction gave the big ghost another opportunity to attack. He pummeled her face, slamming her in the mouth with his fist while he held the back of her head steady with his other hand so she couldn't fall away from him.

Some of Mr. Shadow's teeth broke and fell from her mouth, and the sound of crunching bone and cartilage preceded her nose flattening against her face and her right eye caving in.

Shane and James held back, not interested in aiding either one of the spirits. It seemed for a time like Cassius' brother had the upper hand, but Shadow was not out of tricks.

When the big ghost took her by the throat and lifted her to meet his eyes, Shane saw he had made a grievous mistake even though the ghost had not noticed.

"I want you to scream before you die," the big ghost growled.

The darkness that had replaced Mr. Shadow's arm solidified.

"I want to hear you beg," he continued.

The darkness formed a single blade. Long and then like a machete, curved at the tip.

"I want—"

There was no end to the ghost's final taunt. Mr. Shadow swept her arm from left to right, and the shadow blade sliced cleanly through the bigger ghost's head, removing the top of his skull just below the eyes.

She hung there for a moment in his grip, and then Cassius' brother exploded outward. Shane and James were pushed back, and Mr. Shadow was hurled across the room against the wall. She landed roughly, and Shane watched as the shadows swirling around her receded into her form, leaving her there with a single arm once again as she got to her feet unsteadily.

James was first to the door. He pulled it open, one hand trying to cover the worst of the wounds on his chest, and then stumbled back. A pair of Hounds waited on the other side, with two more behind them.

"There's nowhere to go," Mr. Shadow said. "I told you both you would die, and I keep my word."

"Keep them bottlenecked," Shane said to James. "Hold them off as long as you can."

James swung the iron baton at the Hounds. The metal weapon passed through both ghosts at the door, sending them back to whatever cell they came from. The second two came forward, and James swung again as Shane turned his back on his friend and made a break for Mr. Shadow.

The ghost was fully formed now, more than she had ever been. No shadows swirled at her feet, there was only her as she had been in the illusory memory Shane had seen in Rhode Island.

She had spread herself too thin. Fighting against Shane, dealing with Cassius' brother, and pushing her abilities to the limits had taken its toll. She was weak, missing an arm, and too arrogant to realize she would do better to retreat and regroup.

Shane slipped the iron rings from his fingers, placing them back in his pockets. He didn't want to give Mr. Shadow an out this time. If he and James were going to get away, there was only one path.

He tackled Mr. Shadow, diving for her waist and dragging her to the ground. The ghost had not expected the attack, and it briefly gave Shane the upper hand as he took her by the hair and slammed her head into the ground, scrambling onto her back and keeping her face-down.

She struggled beneath him, and he pounded her head into the ground again and again, using his other hand to land blows to her back and sides. She reached back with her one good hand, jabbing at Shane with pointed fingers, but he avoided the awkward attacks and continued the work Cassius' brother had started, pummeling her face.

Despite her weakened state and vulnerable position, Mr. Shadow was still powerful. Shane's attacks did not have the desired effect. He tried to slam his elbow into the back of her head in the hopes of crushing bone and breaking through, but he couldn't.

Shadow pushed up suddenly, knocking Shane off-balance. He fell to his side and Shadow scrambled on top of him, bringing her knife fingers down into his shoulder as he tried to get away.

He yelled in pain as they pierced his flesh. Shadow wound back for a second blow but Shane hit her hard enough in the face that she fell over, giving him time to get up and defend himself.

"Do you think you'll survive this?" Shadow asked, getting to her feet as well. Her face was crushed, the features distorted beyond recognition. The orbital bones, her jaw, everything was broken but not enough that Shane could end her. She was unrecognizable, but she pushed on.

"Do you?" Shane asked.

Shadow laughed.

"I need not even waste the effort."

She snapped her fingers, and more Hounds pushed through the walls. James backed away from the door, joining Shane as the creatures came at them from all sides, circling the room and closing in.

Shadow laughed once more, cold and triumphant, and the eyeless faces of her servants turned to her. Teeth chattered in lipless mouths and others responded, clicking and clacking as the broken, disfigured monsters closed in.

One of them leaped, but not at Shane or James. Mr. Shadow had backed toward them to use them as a buffer. But the nearest of the Hounds attacked, dragging her to the ground.

"No!" she shouted, struggling away from the creature. Another joined it, pulling at her hand as she forced the first Hound away.

They were all focused on Mr. Shadow now. She was struggling and drawing their attention while Shane and James stood still. Shane knew they focused on targets as a pack, just as they had when he fought Beatrix's brother on the beach.

The Hounds attacked any target they didn't know, Shane realized. And now Shadow, devoid of her shadowy cover, her face damaged beyond recognition, was something unknown to them as well.

A handful of Hounds became a dozen. All of them set upon her, biting, and pulling at her arms, legs, and even her face. As powerful as she was, Mr. Shadow could not contend with the numbers she had brought down on herself.

"Go," Shane said, pushing James to the door. His friend left swiftly while Shane waited behind. He couldn't risk leaving if Shadow was still whole. He had to make sure she was done.

The ghost screamed and raged at the Hounds, but they did not listen to her commands. They tore at her darkened flesh, pulling bits away here and there. Shane saw one tear off her leg, and another finally removed her good hand and her last line of defense, the blade-like fingers vanishing as the hand dissolved.

One of the Hounds lunged at Shadow's already ruined face, plunging a hand into the broken remains and pulling. It was the final blow, the last her form could withstand. Her body exploded with a savage force that sent the assembled Hounds across the room and knocked Shane to the ground in the doorway.

The house shook, and the light in the ceiling flickered and died, plunging Shane into darkness. Shadow was gone and Shane was alone.

He got to his feet and left, catching James halfway down the hall.

EPILOGUE

Shane couldn't see beyond what was in front of him. He kept his left hand on James' back as he guided the man down the dark, damp hallway. He faintly heard sirens somewhere in the distance. There were thumps through the floors, muffled and dull, definitely the sound of people walking on the floor above them.

"I think something is following us," James said.

Shane ignored it. Better to have something follow them up into the light than worry about it down there.

They had reached the central hub. The stone steps were there, and they made their way toward them in the blackness, fumbling with hands and a half-memory of how the staircase looked. The crack under the door at the top let in enough light that he could make out the set of stairs that headed up.

"Can you make it up?" Shane asked.

"I'd climb the wall to the bloody roof if I had to," the older man answered.

Shane released him and took the stairs as quickly as he could, slamming into the door at the top with his shoulder.

Something clicked in the darkness behind them, and Shane turned, looking down the steps to the cellar. The light coming under the door was faint, but he had been in the dark long enough that his eyes had adjusted. He saw one of the Hounds down there, its teeth chattering as it stared up at Shane and James with its empty eyes and skinned face.

"They're not going to stop," James said.

"They will," Shane countered. Anything would stop if you destroyed it.

The Hounds that had survived would escape. They would run off, wild and in a panic. They would eventually regroup; most would probably return to the house. Once they realized no one was there to control them, they would either remain feral, dangerous things, or perhaps some would try to reclaim their humanity. They would all be deadly, though.

Something would need to be done about them. The things they had become were monstrous. Shane was not above a live-and-let-live attitude with most ghosts, but that could not be the case here. It was akin to letting the Dark Ones loose in a forest and hoping that no one would disturb them. Someone would eventually find them and pay the price. But that was a concern for another time.

Shane heard the sirens outside. Agent Ventura had called in more backup. There would be too many eyes around, and he'd cause too much of a scene if he did anything. The Hounds might force his hand. They weren't governed by the principles of tact and discretion. If they attacked law enforcement and the FBI outside, Shane would do what had to be done. Ventura could worry about how to explain it to everyone.

If it came to that.

The Hound at the bottom of the stairs had still not taken a step toward them. Shane wondered if perhaps there was more humanity in them than it seemed. The one watching them seemed to know enough to not want to expose itself to more danger. Hiding in the shadows was the best course of action for any spirit. In Shane's mind, that just made things worse.

Shane slammed his shoulder into the locked door at the top of the stairs again, shaking the frame. The Hound chattered its teeth, rose on its haunches, and then sat again. It reminded Shane of a dog being tested by its owner. The sort where it's shown a snack, but it's been trained to sit still until given permission to eat.

Another hit with all his weight behind it, and the door finally broke open, allowing Shane and James out into the house. Light spilled into the basement, and Shane watched the Hound back away. With so much of its face stripped away, it was hard to say it showed any signs of humanity or intelligence, but something was there. An understanding. It would survive longer if it stayed away from Shane and the others.

A series of gunshots rang out, and Shane and James hit the deck on instinct. The shooter was not near them or targeting them, but neither wanted to catch a stray round.

Someone shouted commands and more gunfire erupted outside. Shane heard glass breaking not far from their position, and he headed in the opposite direction with James on his heels.

"Sounds like a combat zone," the older man said.

"Harvesters picked a fight," Shane guessed.

They made their way to the end of the hallway, and Shane peered around the corner to the front foyer of the house. The door had been broken off its hinges, and two bodies lay on the floor, face-down in blood. Both Harvesters.

"Hands!"

The voice was loud and full of fear. It came from behind, down the hallway from which they'd just fled. Shane raised his hands without turning his head, and James did the same.

Rapid footsteps approached, and a man in black tactical gear emblazoned with the words "Federal Agent" across his back loomed, the barrel of a semiautomatic rifle trained on Shane's face.

"On the ground," the agent said.

"We're not with them," James said. The agent turned his gun on James.

"Kiss the floor. Now."

Shane did not want to get shot by a nervous FBI agent after everything he'd just survived, and opted to acquiesce for now. The sound of gunfire continued to ring out in the near distance, and there were Hounds on the loose. It was not a safe place to get taken prisoner.

"Two suspects in the front hallway, need backup," the agent said into a shoulder microphone.

"We're not suspects," James said with his face on the cold tile. "They tried to kill us."

"Shut up," the agent said. A scratchy reply to his backup call came over the radio, but Shane couldn't make it out. A shotgun blast near the front door caused the agent to turn in a near panic and open fire.

Shane resisted the urge to run or try for the agent's weapon. He was the good guy here; he needed to be smart.

"Shane? James?"

Shane lifted his head. Ventura stepped over the body of a Harvester. He kneeled and checked the pulse of the man who'd just taken a shotgun blast to the chest, leaving him quickly when it was clear he was dead.

"Ullman, these two are with me. They were taken hostage by the cult; there must be more inside," Ventura said to the agent who had stopped Shane and James.

"There are torture victims in the basement," Shane added.

"Jesus Christ, Ventura, you said these were a handful of cranks in the woods."

"I said 'probably'," Ventura corrected. "Clear the basement."

The other agent shook his head and radioed for backup. Shane and James got to their feet. The gunfire had ended outside. There was still shouting, and Shane saw flashing lights through the windows and open door, but the mayhem seemed to be over.

"This was a goddamn nightmare," Ventura said. He looked at James and the wounds across his chest and shoulders and winced. "Come with me."

"You think so?" Shane asked. "I've been having a great time."

He followed Ventura outside. The agent ushered them past a cadre of other agents and Vermont state police toward an ambulance.

"These men were taken hostage. I need you to check them out,"

Ventura told the paramedic.

"Ventura—" Shane began. He had no interest in going through a medical check or being sent back to a hospital.

"You're getting cleared because you are a hostage rescued from a dangerous cult, as will be fully detailed in my report that explains everything that happened here, sir," the agent told him.

Shane sighed and nodded, leaning against the ambulance while the paramedic tended to James.

"Yes sir, Mr. Agent. Thank you for saving us," Shane said.

Ventura shook his head and left swiftly, shouting orders to others. Shane would play nice for Ventura's benefit. He could only imagine how the case would be explained to his superiors. That said, when they found the bodies and Ventura got the praise for cracking what was arguably the worst case of serial killing in the state and maybe the country's history, Ventura would probably earn himself a little leniency.

To Shane's minor delight, the paramedics ignored him when it was clear his injuries were not as pressing as James'. They took the older man into the back of the ambulance and set about dressing his wounds to stop the bleeding.

✳✳✳

The FBI rescued forty-six victims from the basement. Only five survived with minimal injury; more than twenty would never walk or speak again. Mr. Shadow and the Houndmaster had been brutal in their process, and only the ones they'd barely started in on had a chance of survival. It was better than dying and becoming a Hound, though. Even if Shane, James, and Ventura were the only ones who knew what those people had escaped, it was better.

Shane went with the paramedics to the hospital and was given a thorough exam. When they realized the bulk of his injuries were sustained before he even got into the house, they were less adamant about him spending the night. He convinced them to discharge him after just a few hours.

Ventura came by the hospital to check in on Shane and James. The house in the woods was still being searched. They were turning up dead bodies all around the property and throughout the building. It was worse than Shane and Ventura had imagined when they first discovered it.

"It had been going on for years, Ryan," Ventura said. "Before the Houndmaster, I think it was just Shadow trying his luck. Hundreds of bodies. No one at the bureau has ever seen anything like it. People who haven't seen it won't even believe it."

"At least it's over," Shane said.

That was only partially true. There were still a few loose Hounds out there. The house was secluded, but their haunted items could be moved, taken as evidence by the authorities, and transported to a facility as evidence or buried as remains. Shane would have to make sure Ventura kept tabs.

"Yeah," Ventura said, not sounding like he believed it.

"You find stuff like this sometimes. You lift a rock, and it's not a bug underneath, it's a doorway straight to hell. You find monsters."

"Have you seen anything worse than this?" the agent asked him.

Shane thought about the question for a moment. It was hard to answer. Worse was a subjective term. In terms of death, he had not. Mr. Shadow was a plague.

"Don't start ranking horrors. It'll drive you crazy," Shane said finally.

"That's not what's driving me crazy," Ventura replied.

He stared out the window of the hospital room at the parking lot, the city beyond, and the forest in the distance. Shane waited for him to finish his thought.

"I can't help but think of what everyone in the office has been saying. Worst thing they've ever seen. Highest body count they've ever seen.

People must have said that before, right?"

He turned and looked at Shane, who shrugged.

"I assume so," he agreed.

Ventura nodded.

"Something before this was the worst thing anyone ever saw. And something before that was. And before that. So, what comes after this one? What's still waiting out there? Mr. Shadow had only been around for a few decades. What about the ghosts of people who died a thousand years ago? Five thousand years ago? What if one of them has been doing stuff like this the whole time? Are we going to run into that one day?"

Shane didn't have an answer. He didn't want to tell Ventura that he'd met ghosts that old and had seen some of the horrors they could commit. Maybe there was something worse than Mr. Shadow, something that made her pale in comparison. But what good would worrying about it do?

"Don't drive yourself crazy, Ventura. Not worth it."

"What do I do, then?"

"Have a smoke. Have a cup of coffee. Get a good night's sleep. The world will be here tomorrow."

He said a quick goodbye to James before heading out. He reminded his friend to call the waitress from Syracuse when he felt up to it, then left.

He needed to get home and take his own advice. A smoke in the garden, a quick coffee, and some of that sleep he'd been putting off for far too long.

※

Check out these best-selling series from our talented authors:

GHOST STORIES

RON RIPLEY
BERKLEY STREET SERIES
MOVING IN SERIES
HAUNTED COLLECTION SERIES
DEATH HUNTER SERIES

IAN FORTEY
JIGSAW OF SOULS SERIES
CULT OF THE ENDLESS NIGHT SERIES

SUPERNATURAL SUSPENSE

A. I. NASSER
SLAUGHTER SERIES
SIN SERIES

DAVID LONGHORN
NIGHTMARE SERIES
ASYLUM SERIES

SARA CLANCY
THE BELL WITCH SERIES
BANSHEE SERIES

For a complete list of our new releases and best-selling horror books, visit
ScareStreet.com or scan the QR code below!

www.ingramcontent.com/pod-product-compliance
Lightning Source LLC
Chambersburg PA
CBHW050345030726
47503CB00008B/2624